Dearest Ma

There are no lie lit

this dream of false love

There are only which have

perceptions — yet to be filled with

love.

THE SILENT PARTNER

And Other Stories Of Truth

JULIET CASTLE
Illustrated by Jaye Gray

Copyright © 2017 Juliet Castle

The moral right of the author has been asserted.
All images copyright Jaye Gray

Apart from any fair dealing for the purposes of research or private study, or criticism or review, as permitted under the Copyright, Designs and Patents Act 1988, this publication may only be reproduced, stored or transmitted, in any form or by any means, with the prior permission in writing of the publishers, or in the case of reprographic reproduction in accordance with the terms of licences issued by the Copyright Licensing Agency. Enquiries concerning reproduction outside those terms should be sent to the publishers.

Matador
9 Priory Business Park,
Wistow Road, Kibworth Beauchamp,
Leicestershire. LE8 0RX
Tel: 0116 279 2299
Email: books@troubador.co.uk
Web: www.troubador.co.uk/matador
Twitter: @matadorbooks

ISBN PB:978 1785898 938
HB: 9781785899058

British Library Cataloguing in Publication Data.
A catalogue record for this book is available from the British Library.

Printed and bound by CPI Group (UK) Ltd, Croydon, CR0 4YY
Typeset in 11pt Minion Pro by Troubador Publishing Ltd, Leicester, UK

Matador is an imprint of Troubador Publishing Ltd

To my silent partner

Contents

Foreword – From the J.C. Love Letter Desk
xi

Introduction – The Prepared One
xv

The Silent Partner
1

My Father's Hands
5

Sandbox
8

The Prize Fighter
11

A Woman Who Had Three Sons
13

Second Nature
23

He Said
27

My Sister's Friend
29

Without a Rocking Chair
34

Victory
37

Ripples in Circles
39

Forgiveness When the Sun Wanes and the Moon
Shines
42

When I Awoke
46

The Place
48

Absurd
51

Easy Street
54

Richard's Farm
55

The Earth Roars
59

Hazy Affection
62

The Steed
66

Hosting Colour
68

Oar
71

The Black Panther
76

Reaching Riches
79

The Last Hallway
81

Bothersome
85

A Musk Deer
88

Eskew
91

Pardon Me, But I Love You
94

The Donkey
97

Something of Substance
99

Catering
104

Clueless
106

Higher Ground
109

Ticket Master
112

The Twilight Hour
117

Merci
119

Pensive
123

A Fisherman's Tale
127

Eventually
130

Just Paint
133

Rose
136

The Carpenter's Son
139

Trading Places
142

Living the Dream
145

Lila the Lily
148

Serenity
151

Eye
154

Epilogue – An Offering
157

The Author
159

The Artist
160

With Gratitude
161

From the J. C. Love Letter Desk
(Foreword)

I see a story. It embraces me. It plays out its intimacies in a scene, before my mind, with all its intricacies. The slightest subtleties are noticed. Every element shines. I feel its power.

Often sad, the tales of life are. Because we are out of sync with ourselves. Uncomfortable. Unsettled. Grieving for some strong foundation, so we can trust. Uneasy, we are. Diseased.

We want to please. All of us. We all want to please all of us. But it doesn't seem to work. Because it doesn't. We're insensitive to each other and have become so sensitive to others. And oversensitive to ourselves. It's a living hell.

I write the stories as they relay. They play out succinctly. Will anyone capture the rapture I see in their scenes? The misery of uncomfortable human nature? Will anyone notice?

I do. I see it in all of us. The smallness of us wanting to be big. So out of sorts. Can't sort it out. Just small bits, but none of it really matters. It's kind of sickening, but oh, so much good comes to the plight upon discovery.

I want to tell the tale of the etheric stories that I see, the images of people's lives flashed before my eye. How I see them, acting out their lives, trying, spending time, living. These snaps of moments capture the whole of people's lives. All of it is seen within their responses, their twitches, their behaviours. All of it is there. You can decipher it without hardly trying, if you care to.

Lost in the awkwardness of the situation, of relationships, of emotional bliss and its spiralling lows, of catastrophe, of exaggeration, of travesty, tragedy, accidents, nonsense. Lost.

I see the inside of these lives, and I surmise that somewhere deep we all just want to love.

I see compassion. Compassion for blundering. For wanting. For giggling. For acceptance. For cruelty. For seeking. For culture. For celebration, for misfortune and for all the hardship of just being free to choose amongst life's challenging rules. I see compassion. It seeps into me, and I want to free every one of the players in the images of the stories of life. I see the people acting out their scenes with such intent. I want to free them, to let them know about their soul. It is waiting for them to let go, so it can explode into the cosmos again.

From love comes peace.

I love you all.

THE SILENT PARTNER
And Other Stories of Truth

Him that overcometh will I make a pillar in the temple of my God, and he shall go no more out.

—Revelations 3:12

The Prepared One
(Introduction)

This book is about laughter, sorrow, life and Spirit. But most of all, it is about courage – the courage to see where you are on the continuum of your life's journey. Where is your marker in your book of life? And beyond that, where, how, and when will you choose to go forward from here?

I invite you to listen to how you may want to go forward, to choose on your own. Let me plot the course. Allow me to.

Let yourself go within, as you go within this book. Let go, yet remain keenly aware. Allow yourself the privilege of seeing where it may take you.

It will take you somewhere. Somewhere different. Somewhere the same. Where you remember something. Something the same and yet new. Déjà vu.

You may not comprehend the way you're used to. But you will understand. Yourself. This opening. This explosion into yourself that recognizes something. It is there. Present.

These words will find that door inside and open it a little, or much, depending on how you allow it. It is waiting for your generosity. You are.

In this trial, you will choose the best road for you. By this choice, you can open the possibility to return to be the Lord of your own vessel. Here, you meet the Silent Partner.

The Silent Partner

I am the Silent Partner. The writer, the creator, the fuel behind the players. The one directing the scene. The performers take the bows, the celebrations in their honour for their successes.

I am the Silent Partner. The witness to all that played out to get here, wherever here may be. I have no need for drama, no desire for credits. I only need to see the scenes being seen, to see the reflection of my work as it is illuminated in *others*.

I am the Silent Partner. The closer my associates get to me, or know of me, the more aligned our business will run. They come together thinking they are running the show, exchanging niceties and donning garments of disguise, to be the seller and the buyer, the banker and the borrower, the father and the son. But it is I behind every exchange. They know it is I, but in so much freedom of making their own way, they sell themselves the belief that it is they who are the show; that there could be no show without them.

But there is no business without the funding from the Silent Partner. There is only a storefront, with mannequins and cut-out dolls. There is no backer, no backbone, no spine to the business that makes it run. All the frivolities are topped on the base of the substance that supports it.

I am the Silent Partner. You see me when you are woeful, at times when you are sincerely looking. But in me you see strength; it scares you. You will need to drop your pretences to approach me, and you know that I will see through your knitted disguise simply by looking into your eyes. You do not approach. You would rather reproach. You are afraid of seeing what you know to be true. You are not prepared to meet your maker. You are not prepared to say that it is not you who strings the puppet. You are not brave enough to say you are the one whose voice was ringing in the chatter of all that didn't matter, and how you wooed and woed to make it so.

You are not funny enough yet. You are not yet laughing from the heart. You are not yet bursting with brilliance. You are not yet done. You are not ready to approach the Silent Partner, to thank him for all he has fuelled for you, for his ideas that you've claimed, for his fame that you've named. He is not distressed at your disguise or demise. He clothed you, did he not? He gave you bread and butter and milk – to "milk". He does not want to be centre stage. He does not want to be the one standing when the curtain falls. He has it all.

He is the Silent Partner because this is who he is. He knows about all that glows. He sent it out, with ribbons and bows. It is you who are still waiting for the show to go on, when the curtain falls. It is you who believes there must be yet another scene. He knows it's all from in-between. He is the creator of the scene, the writer, the fuel behind the fire, that of endless desire. He enjoys the show, however it goes. He has no need for fame. He is always the same, the Silent Partner.

The Silent Partner

My Father's Hands

Into my Father's hands I was placed. The comfort of his agility bouncing through me, the pillar of his strength forming my young spine into backbone.

He is as a temple. A temple made of rocks, rumbled into place by great Grace.

My Father's hands: carved. Courageous. Occupied with love and land and earth beneath his feet. I love him, my Father. The Father in him. I love him adoringly, pouringly, without limit or understanding. Without need.

He picks up the plough from the ground and moves the earth that separates to welcome the seeds of life. He tends. He laughs. He frees the joy from the tension, and it explodes into the day. He lights the moon on fire, and it glows in coolness.

He wraps me in his coat and buttons it loosely like a big belly. I giggle quietly, so tickled to be special. I am locked inside of him, and he is mine for this time. I giggle. I'm tickled at how fine this is. My Father's hands hold me close, and his eyes twinkle with mischievous love in the play of it all. I love him adoringly, pouringly, with all of me wrapped into him.

He releases me and says, "Run." It means free. He gives me wings where I was once only a carrot seed. I want only to grow my roots so I can be at home, kept close to him, held in his hands and wrapped in his belly.

He says, "Run!" again. "Fast. Run fast, little one. Your time has come."

His hands release me, and all the glory within them comes. The warmth, the strength, the comforting embrace. It stretches to me and sticks to me like glue, and I am stuck to the floor. I can run no more. Not any. All I want to do, all I can do, is be still in the glow of my Father's hands.

But then a nudge from the gentle giant, and I tip a step. The beam of sunrays lights my way, the magic of my Father's ways embossed within my inner me. Like stepping into the sea with neon lights of fireflies glued on your shoes, I dance the next prance. He smiles at me, the free me, and pats my back lovingly. I take it with me, the pat, and it glows within my step. I have my Father's magic. I am amazed at my feat. But deep inside, I do surmise that it is a gift from him to me.

I count the fingers on my hands, the five great forces of dexterity. I am the next to sow the land; the future lies here with me. What will I put into the soil? Will it be green to grow? And like my Father's steps into the dirt, which way will I direct the plough to go?

I will not rest till this is done – the fun, the work, the day. Into my bed; the sun is down. Into my Father's hands I'll stay.

Sandbox

My mother calls, and I hear her whisper from deep within. Give me a bone to lay my tension around, that it may have something to hold it that is stronger than me.

I wanted to cry, to laugh, to be melancholy, to holler to the heavens to pick me up from here and take me to places I know exist and more so. Thrivingly alive.

I wanted to live in a story with trolls and goblins that walk alongside angels and nymphs, but all that came was this.

Today I dance into the trance of her arms, a place so make-believe and unpredictable, its falsehood nearly puts me into misery. We frolic in the playfulness of the awaiting atomic bomb that is lit, then out, then lit, then out, then lit, then not a worry.

I gather my resources to take stock of the remainder of the game. Do I have enough to play it, and how will I play it so I have enough? A whisper of hair falls from the circle of my ear. I flush with anxious knowing of the undoing of the rest of me.

Collapse. It comes so that I may breathe again. A shiny chain dangles from the tree of life, and I think it fills the space between its branches, but I don't know how. I waste my sight looking harder to see. Be the one that presents itself without confusion, please. Be the easy knowing. The chain drops, and when I pick it up, it's tied in tiny knots that seem impossible to have been constructed from where it's been – nowhere. And yet it is bundled to its breaking point.

I am the little girl who plays in the sandbox, some sand, some dirt. I think they see me here hidden among the scrubby shrubs. They want to see me. I want them to see me. They want me to be unseen, to be hidden. I want to be hidden, invisible to them.

I go into the house. Quietly.

The Silent Partner

The Prize Fighter

He placed his hand into the cup and drew out the soaking sponge. It sapped its savour of healing into the wound, the hole in his heart.

I am the Warrior, he said. I am unscathed except by the wounds that make me believe I am mortal. Falsely. I am immortality.

I am the destroyer of the mind, till it waves its white flag in surrender to a new state, a clean slate. I am the ambush of your emotions, till they pine or whine no more, their resilience achieved.

Fear not my sword, for it bears only truth as its fruit. It kills only that which lies in the way of the living, that which is already a corpse. It seeks only justice, in fair exertion. It performs only well, cutting madness from mainstream, hysteria from home. Health be its only survivor.

I am the Warrior, he said. Be not afraid. I bring the casualties of war to your feet as a prize for your taking, a token of my task. Into your palm I press my blood, the circle of life, from my white horse to your home, from my heart to your master.

May the wings of doves bring news of the wounds of battle forever healed by the light rider who was not deterred by false pretences or swayed by casualties. Freedom comes at a price and brings its prize, the Warrior said.

A Woman Who Had Three Sons
(Part One)

There once was a woman who had a daughter and three sons. Each of her three sons died. The first, born early and out of wedlock, was given away for adoption. To the woman, this was the death of her son. She gave him wholeheartedly and in the name of love, and in that she considered it final, like a death.

The second son was never born. She miscarried him, and he died in his eighth week in her womb.

The third son she knew well, and he lived until a month short of manhood at sixteen. She mourned heavily in her heart, and she called to her soul to call to Spirit, that he may be returned to her – partly for mercy in her deep mourning, and partly so she could know that he was being cared for. She begged to the Sky that he was being cared for and walked miles in the day and dark, talking to the heavens, asking that he be okay, that he be guided, loved affectionately, and amused by great teachers. She begged that he not be afraid, that he not be wondering or wandering. She cried to God a thousand, thousand tears. She wanted to see her son, to hear him, to know. Was he okay?

"How will I live without my son?" she asked. "I want my son back. I want my son back." She wrote the words into her journal daily, nightly, in the middle of her sleep, her dreams, her nightmares, her yearnings. Silence was all she felt while the plaguing longing besieged her.

She lay on his bedroom floor at night, in the morning, during the day. She put on his big shoes that had fallen from his feet when the tree stood its ground and the truck bent to surround it. The glass from the windows crushed into crystals and filled his eyes with a glistening stare, when she saw him in the morgue. His million-dollar smile was now filled with crowded teeth crushed by the breaking of his jaw. But all she saw was her beautiful son. Nothing undone.

She felt too small to sleep on the bed anymore. The floor felt grounded like earth, and she laid her pillow down and felt surrounded by depth. She thought about the people of China on the other side of the world doing the same thing beneath her.

She wrote his name in the snow across their backyard, where he used to play hockey until…

"God has abandoned me," she said. "Where is God?"

In her grief, she heard silence and wanted more. She thought all she heard was silence and wanted more – more understanding, more knowing, more communication.

"I will communicate," she said, though she already had. She already was.

Sometimes we fail to see what we already have and what we already are. We are still in the path of the circle. She was seeing the circle.

And out of what seems the greatest misfortune, at times, comes the contrary: to endure the path with the deepest desire for understanding of the heart.

He fled quietly, her son, back to his first home. In the spirit of knowing, she saw him leave and ran to follow him there, but it was not her time. She was left a blessing, a daughter, as milky as snow and innocent as a white rose, to accompany her and, together and apart, they endured.

Screaming filled the house on some occasions. It was a prior stranger to this cosy home. It felt like an invader. On days, still, the house held laughter, often followed by tears. Stranger still, it held silence, welcome and unwelcome. Paradox, paradox, paradox.

The trees talked and showed images in their shadowy branches in the night. The gate creaked open, and she heard him enter. They saw him walk through; they heard him speak.

"I'm okay, Mom," he said. "Hi, Mom. Hi, Jaye."

He was an apparition in the hallway, in the living room. In their dreams he visited them as he was before, and in different ages and stages and places and deaths.

She knew it all to be true. She had heard the knocking of death at her door this time and many times before.

They called him an angel, those who knew him. Those who didn't know him talked like they didn't know him, but had to talk about him still. Because he was the one to talk about.

The TV newswoman said, "He was everyone's son." The people who weren't his brother called him brother, and the ones who weren't his sister. He moved them.

They said he was fast, like a gazelle; he ran without looking like he was running. He was funny in a comical kind of way. He was forgiveness – all of it.

She mourned him because she knew him so well. It was a gift, to mourn for that reason. Such joy in exchange for sorrow.

She wandered and wondered what she needed to see, that she was seeing this?

God left a message saying, "This is God. Leave a message."

"God has a sense of humour. A good one," she said. She laughed when it only seemed appropriate to cry.

She couldn't tell the difference between what was real and what was make-believe, but there was a definitive play that what she once thought was, was not. It put her into shock, even though she knew it all along.

She had forgotten some, not all. Just a distraction of days lulled by the music of the cranky world into a time of distancing. What seemed like years was but a glimpse of the forgotten fortune of sorrow; the real gold at the end of the rainbow.

She started to remember. It was like breaking glass – shards of crystallised prisms with stories hidden inside. Stories from before that were still going on, and stories from now, and stories that you thought you couldn't know yet.

"What does this dream mean?" she asked. "Tell me in the simplest way, because I cannot seem to understand."

"We are all playing roles," God said.

She could not believe he was gone forever, her son, because he was everywhere. He talked to her in the day and welcomed her home at night. She wondered how to mourn the death of a son who wasn't dead. And yet the loss of separation made that easy. The idea of pain made pain, where she knew none could possibly truly exist.

"How can we pretend he is gone when he is still here?" The question of sanity seemed insane. The way of the world became the delusion.

The death of her son became the realisation that he was still living, and in this was gratitude.

"We're just really appreciative we had fifteen years," she told the newswoman who reported when he died.

No one opens up the door that is yet to remain closed.

And there was screaming and agony in the home that had never known either before.

A Woman Who Had Three Sons

(Part Two)

To my darling daughter,

Remember the day that Jarvis died? You alone at home, and I so far away. Partners at our side who are no longer here, replaced now with white knights. The road has been long in duration, in remembering, short in its course. You saw his eyes that day, deeped in kindness, in life and death, the smile that never was truly broken, the laugh that we still hear.

"I'm still here," he says. We can't pretend we don't hear him when he is so loud, as he always was – not to most, and not in the crowd, but simply his presence. It was undeniable and still is. Some things never change. Some things look like they can't stand still when you're always moving.

Pennies from heaven fell everywhere. We only had to think of him or not think of him, and they were there to validate him and remind us. The pennies we hid, while hardly hiding them, amongst the house, so he would find them. He never did.

He saw them first, pennies everywhere. They fell from the sky into his sight, and so gullibly he told you, "Do you notice that there are pennies everywhere?" So we planted them, the seeds of heaven, in every little nook and cranny and open space to tease him. Not one he said he noticed. We picked them up, one by one. Then he passed into the sky and saw what we had done, and more, and he sent them everywhere in our path. A million pennies to match his million-dollar smile.

Love,

Mom

A Woman Who Had Three Sons

(Part Three)

It seemed wicked that night. You told me of the icy rain that came and pretended to warm the icy winter days prior. Icy cold. You stole away to stay longer with a friend, and he was alone with his best. He drove her home, as she desired, the house clean, the bottles recycled, the party undone from the days before. Even the sliver space between the cabinet and the fridge was wiped so all would look renewed before I arrived home.

Oh, O Mexico. A chance trip on the latter half of my sister's vacation. To what do I owe this twist of luck – or fate?

He took her home, and on his return, our corner lot lit in his view, he went sideways. Everything did. Took a right turn into no road and hugged the tree so tight it almost moved. Roots. He left them there: the tree, the glass, the football star, me, you and a mountain of others. He left them there.

The Silent Partner

Second Nature

I didn't care. The things that mattered to most didn't matter to me. Those came easily, except that it was like brute force because I didn't care.

You need to love something to want it. Wholeheartedly, I mean. Not like tinker toys and meagre joys that come from the candy store, where wind-up dolls and toy men who wish they were real shop.

It's so awkward – the feigned affection, the blankness. Someone said something one day, and it got buried deep inside his or her mechanics, and the song kept playing the similar tune. Who put it in there and wound it so tight in the machinery of you? I wish you'd undo, stop for a time. Unwind fully so we could reprogram you. Or keep you new, fresh, clean without the oil. No more greasy handshakes.

Who gave you permission to act this way? Accordingly. According to what you do, what you say. Who do you think you are? Big star?

Shine bright, speck of light.

I wish I had known that this would happen. That I would end up like this, perfectly perfect, instilled in what one might call a moment of time.

It was four o'clock – way past your bedtime and so close to mine. The moon being my watchdog. The sun waking me late in the day.

Solidly, I felt. My feet touched the ground, and it was like dirt, black and cushioned but firm. The kind that grows things. I knew there were earthworms beneath my feet, buried there, making the earth work, making it primed for the season of blossoming. It was perfect, these outside things that were planted in our path. Joining roots, bellowing howls of wind, animals loping in the night when everyone slept. But I made my day.

I couldn't make it form the way I wanted to. Not wanted so much as deeply desired. The manufacturing of the world as a beautiful one. It was a mix, actually. A hodgepodge of desire and that same uncaring approach that I possessed. Like wanting to caress the world into something beautiful but understanding it was just as it was, maturing immaturely like a child. Sometimes rotten, spoiled, blatantly bad on purpose. Sometimes learning hard lessons through years of tears. And sometimes so innocent and wise at the same time, a speck of light that illuminates everything in the dark sky at night. When I am awake and everyone sleeps.

Who told them to sleep during the night? Who told them it was right? Who told them it was all right, okay, that they had permission?

I wanted to go away. To a place where they all were, and it wasn't them. The ones who roll their eyes and then keep going till they are the New Year's Eve party favours that whistle when you blow them in your mouth as they unravel and strut and fluff their feathers out in a shrill thrill. Rolling out and in again till it gets crumpled, and then you toss it aside for a new toy. A temporary one.

I didn't want you to go away. I just wanted you to be perfect again. Not even like I wanted it, or cared, but more like I loved you, when I thought of you that way. Perfectly perfect. Flawed, in natural beauty, intently staring back at me. Trying to do without knowing how, but figuring it out after scratching your head and laughing out loud.

I loved you to stay up at night – not all night, but just the best part. When the silence fell and the dew came when we weren't looking, and then it was suddenly there, and we were chilled together. Chillin' together. Looking at the moon and just loving how awesome it struck, like a speck of brilliant light in the dark night. We could hear the earthworms crawl in the silence and the bats bat their eyes, wondering why we were up here so late with them, and not caring, but loving us to be with them too.

We'd be quiet, sharing thoughts – the big kinds that stay with you till you see their magnitude as a part of you. The ones you remember when you thought of them, where you were on that night, and how it lingered with you for the days and stages that followed. Till you saw it shine on your pillow one night on your last sleep of sleeps, and you gave it permission to leave. And you closed your eyes, and the day didn't wake you because you didn't really care, and neither did you want it to, but you loved it all.

I give you permission to live.

He Said

"Away with the world," he said. "Toss it away with the waves on the ocean, and watch it float on by and then back. You are the dictator of your story, the wave of delight that you manifest outward. It can crash on the shore and then return back to you. The message in the wave doesn't change depending on its crash or lull. Only those who want to see the excitement of the crash see the message there, and those who want to see it in the lull, see it in the lull.

"Duality. Both are the same while appearing to represent differently to the untrained mind.

"You walk in the woods, and the angels sing and answer your song. You hear them; you converse. Do not pretend it is not so. It is so. They grant you the story of you, and you hear and translate it well and with concise articulation. Leave the doubt alone in its petty place. That which you endeavour through *Thy will be done*, will be done. You see obstacles so small in relation to the obstacles of seeing your story and chanting its message. The latter, you are.

"The words are written. Tell your tale. Spin it into its divine tapestry, which only you know the work."

Blessed be thy name.

My Sister's Friend

He began to look at me in a way that made me notice. I could feel the intimacy of the exchange in a way worth noticing. A way that I wasn't used to, except in few and far instances that I could count on one hand. On the other hand, I couldn't remember them, only the familiar touching of it now that I missed somehow. I missed it dearly, the feeling of intimacy.

I raced to the road to watch him go. The lane curved, sidestepped, in sight and out of sight. I sidestepped myself to see, hurrying to get to the curve's edge so I wouldn't miss him. Though I already was. Missing him.

We had the nicest time. We dined. We sat quietly. I wish he had been there for me. I wish he had been waiting for me. She never came. Well, she appeared for a moment but wasn't here presently. She didn't see the need. There wasn't one in his eyes. He was self-sufficient. Self-contained. Restrained in the nicest way. The kind of avenue that makes you want to travel to the place you see within him.

I didn't care to be discouraged. That he was only here for a short while. That he didn't get to see her, much, only briefly. That was all he needed without needing anything. I was the recipient of the greatest kind, the one surprised by the meeting of him and me, without even having put out a desire. It came so naturally, like a fallen leaf that lands at your feet when it could have gone anywhere. Everywhere.

I didn't expect the stance he took. The gentle hook that caught the fish but left it reeling. Taking the line out with it, so it could meet its maker whenever it simply surrendered. Yet there was no need to do so. Just upon its choosing. I saw how much she mattered to him, yet no different than a stranger. All, a companion to him. They all thought they were, like I did, intimate with him on our first meeting. Simply a greeting was the nature of our first meeting.

I thought she was fortunate to know him more. My sister. How fortunate to have him call for her, call to her, call on her. Almost as if it was something that had blossomed with attachment. But I knew better. I knew he simply had that way that made you want to have him stay. It was better this way. This casual elegance caught in intimacy that awakened the human heart in me; that spun me to infinity. I wished it would last for eternity.

My sister's friend was a man of calibre. Ticking like the precision of a clock. Swiss made. This time spent with him reminded me of the times I held myself at bay, keeping myself hidden from the overexposure of the world, the talking maladies that tried to decipher melody amongst heavy metal and call it musical. Today I heard the symphony sung in a simple greeting. I kept its tune within my skull and followed it along till he was gone. Watching him go, into the curves and out again, around the bends into the straightaway – I was never the same. I remembered his name. I remembered the moment he came. I remembered his look, his stare, and the intimacy of his care. I tied a ribbon around my finger so I would always remember the stranger who came to visit my sister. My sister's friend.

A white crane lands upon the dock where I sit on the lawny bottom of our house. It crooks its head and preens its down a bit. It glances at me fragilely, skinny neck and feet that land so lightly to meet me here, to greet me here. I see in its eyes a creature's disguise of instinct that makes it cast its way. It doesn't differentiate. It keeps its pace in store with what it chooses to see based on its decree. I am no different to it. Though I am not a fish, I am no different than something that's simply different. I want to feel something stir within it, but it is absent, while filling the void with the nature of itself. I feel the emptiness of intimacy, the greeting between him and me. Simply. Succinctly. Elegantly.

I rock on the dock as my sister approaches. Her scant feet dance across the timber slats.

She says, "How ya doing?" So matter-of-fact. The crane lifts its chin and takes flight in the wind. She sits beside me. Peacefully.

Instead of dread filling my head in the days I thought of like this, I felt the calm of a time bygone, one that I remembered with bliss. I wanted to cry, but not a tear came to my eye in the beauty of those here today. I looked at the ribbon upon my ring finger and realised this feeling would stay. This was the day they took her away. This was the day my sister went away. The undertaker helped her to flee. And on this wood dock, a crane came to watch as I spread her remains to the sea.

The Silent Partner

Without a Rocking Chair

I sat on the porch and cried. He found me there. He rocked me. Without a rocking chair. I lipped the words to my favourite song, *Rock-a-Bye Baby*, all along.

He was the man I never knew. Not father, son, or brother. The man of feigned disguise, the three of them together. I surmised I would die at this very awakening. The sunlight in his eyes, the daylight breaking.

I walked on to the doorway; a squeak it made upon my entry. It had been so long ago, when I had stumbled from its landing. But then I saw inside, the grassy meadows barren. The same I saw outside, ne'er they were ill forgotten.

The woes I cried on the porch were soothed by my stranger's hand. Soft and sweet and heavily calloused, like the feeling of a man. I took a step into the doorway while he sat still on the porch step. He watched me enter steadily but made no move to interject. I wondered for a moment how I deserved this twist of fate. This loyal steed beside me, calmly watching me enter the gate.

I know without recognition that his presence here was needed – rather, all that was ever needed all along. Though wolves or vermin stalked along the outskirts of this porch, he alone would calmly sit, and they would not employ. With the sword he held inside him, one was not needed in a sheath. Not weapons or battalion, just his strength for all to see.

I entered through the gate, the doorway, thresholding the same. And in he followed me, familiar with this play.

The place was filled with strangers that smiled as I swayed through. The greetings of their hearts came shining like ones I must have known. I sank down in my skirt and felt the wonder all around. They parted to simply gesture their acceptance of my dismount.

This lowly place upon the ground was the highest I'd ever been. The stranger who walked beside me, the best friend I'd ever seen. I smiled, a teeny parting of my lips. He understood the meaning and hoisted me upon his hip.

"She's here," he said in gentle tones, yet everyone could hear. "She's come to celebrate the end of all her fame and fear."

I smiled again, the pattern of it embossed upon my mouth. The time I'd spent outside this door was fading quickly now.

The music started, a singing of rhythm in my ears so high and fine. I grinned again, accustoming to this new world of mine.

The Silent Partner

Victory

You have crossed the threshold to infinity, and within it lies everything. The raison d'être.

Its peak, that which you could only imagine, is hidden within the clouds above the highest mountains. Valleys beg to know of its existential bliss while gratefully seeking the warmth of its shelter.

Within the summit of this intelligence, the largest obstacles are but grains of wayward sand. Here, greatest victories are fulfilled.

Small, you are. The peons of neon lights. Pray tell, why do you question the dynamism of this source, while not simply relishing in its mighty essence? Within awestruck abode, you crawl inside its surroundings without moving at all.

Yea, though I walk through the valley of the shadow of death, thou art with me. The rod within you vibrates to connect its magnetic poles through nature's laws and beyond, to the Divinity. To return you there. You are the direction-setter. The staff you choose to guide you is yours alone to choose.

The Silent Partner

Come hither to our table, O wise and wandering one. We embrace you for your travels and your eagerness to learn. Lay down your weapons. Your war is over.

The sage smells sweet beneath your feet. It blossoms into you. Fear not. Take the reins of your chariot and ride your horses into the gates of triumph. Hear the trumpets blow, the bells ring. You have paid the toll to cross the bridge and have seen the troll's disguise.

When sun sets on the third day, you will see your evening rise into day, and the night will be no more except in dreams.

Your mind besieges you. Steady on. The details fall fray within your ideas, cemented by blind thought and senseless action. There are better ways to be your master. Find your volunteers and pay them well, your soldiers, your rowers.

Masked, you stood at your journey's junctures, your road to go unknown. Yet here you stand. Though your skills seem waning, your task is close at hand. Prosperity you seek – that which you already have, and nay, more. New. The awakening of your fallen angel, soon to be.

Close the hand of God, who embraces you within, like a giant who lifts you from your little land into his castle. Here, you see the majesty and never need look back in the same way, or at all. Burn your boat and bridges. Not because you demonstrate you will not return home, but because you know you have returned home, to this new land, the new frontier, with its familiarity like no other.

Ripples in Circles

I went to the water's edge and hung my head over. There was no shampoo, but this soap would do. It had been days since I was washed, and I tossed my hair into the water. It was warm, natural and warm. No green algae. Only ripples in circles coming backwards from me.

Somehow this all made sense, being out here, doing this thing with the birds and the bees and the trees. I felt like them. Buzzing, flying, standing still. Perfectly still. Listening to the birds and the bees. Letting, hoping they would land on me.

Some might say it was lonely in these woods, but for me, it felt darn good. I was going to stay for a while. I wasn't planning on it. There was no plan. No plans were made on these kinds of lands. I was gonna stay, I decided spontaneously, and cast it in stone that I skipped on the water.

Seven times. The ripples spiralled into each other like concentric orbits of time that followed some predetermined strategy that no one understood. It felt good. To watch it. To see it organise. Here, in the woody woods where things grew and decayed and changed to stay that way. Cycles in circles. Keeping time.

I came back to the wash and my scrubbed scalp and the freshness of smell. The wet, the warm, the water tempted me and I didn't resist. Stripped. Naked, into the water I went. Head to toes.

I was a diver since young. It was a passion that washed my cares away, sitting on the dock. Erasing time. Singing in my mind. Spending overtime washing my underarms, sipping dirty water and squirting it in mouthfuls at my beau. Take that, Romeo! Till he overthrew me, and into the wild wet I went. Whoopee!

Those weren't better days. They were good, like today. Like all these, spending time here in the woods. Being understood. Cooperating with ease. Just me, the trees, the birds and the bees.

The Silent Partner

Forgiveness When the Sun Wanes and the Moon Shines

I sought out revenge. The sweet kind. The kind that slides in, nicely, onto home plate, when others are watching the play on second base. Gently, intentionally, I sought out my revenge, and it landed just where I saw it would fall.

It was sweeter than I thought. Syrupy. The kind that sticks to you, like goo. Oozing into the cracks of its shadowed crevices. Within each one and in-between the lines so fine. They felt it. Each and every one that was involved in my plot. My antagonistic mystery, known only to me.

I didn't want to start out like this. The time we spent together dismissed. By thundering, blundering, I introduced by my dismissal of you. My plan to scheme the end of our dream. But the relationships gone wrong were getting too disturbing. Not in a big sense, just from nonsense.

I didn't want to start out like this. And I didn't. I started out close to you, open to you. But all was misconstrued. I didn't want to start out like this. But I would end it, affecting all of you.

The Silent Partner

I wish I could be in your shoes, to see how you viewed the outside from your insides. Messed up, I thought. You were taught to be mighty in your liberties, taking liberties with me and others you see. I didn't appreciate it. It didn't amuse me. While you clicked your heels, each time I was reeled into your catastrophe that made me want to get a hold of me.

I wanted out. Out of the charade that made me a character fit to play the fool. I didn't care for that character anymore. Or any less. I am funny, for sure. But I care not to be the butt of all your jokes, as a rule.

I stepped aside and watched you poise yourself with pride. Friendships, feignedly sought, had you caught in a circle of exclusion, like you were the reason to be, the centre of the stage. You liked it that way. I came to your exclusive party and didn't see the error of those ways. They affected me, dissecting me into fragments of the whole person I once was. The separation filled my former admiration with a newness of me that could have frozen my mother, should she have witnessed me. I became cold, heartless from watching you mess up my life with your strife. But it wasn't your fault. I became less, and it disjointed me to the place where I couldn't see the goodness in my being anymore. Not with clarity.

I troubled the inside of me till it wouldn't humble me anymore. It said it didn't care. I stared at night while I lay in bed, building scenarios in my head, lining up messes to get myself in. When did this all begin? When I let myself go – to a place where I was okay to make a mistake, as long as it didn't let you break another bone in my body. The soft ones, the ones that kept me walking and talking, while splitting splinters of who I used to be and slivering them inside of me. Pointing sharply at what needed to be done. Knowing that if I decided to run, I'd take your needling with me and wouldn't get very far before it would start to blister in me, remembering the fool I'd been.

I wanted to end what was started. To make a new start. To get ahead of this old route where I'd been shot in the dark without knowing why, and it felt like I'd been shot in my heart from the inside out.

I mooned you and your friends as you sat in disclosure. Making poses for a new day. Talking about idle things when there was nothing juicier to say. You didn't see it coming, and I didn't stop to rest, with my bum sticking out and my – well, you know the rest.

You don't have to imagine how embarrassed you were, awkwardly wondering if what you were seeing was me doing that dirty deed. Sure, it could be misconstrued as fun. You'd laugh at it for days, eventually. But I know what it meant to you and what it meant for me. I wanted to rub it into you, this embarrassment. I was so ashamed of myself for putting up with you.

But it wasn't your fault. I wasn't myself. I'd let my defences down. I'd been okay to be your clown, the butt of your jokes, the silly bloke. I wanted my revenge, and though I felt silly and less than me, I walked home with my head held high and my pants pulled up. My dignity. I wouldn't bend to be your friend anymore. Revenge is sweet when you're incomplete.

But I'm now the one that I once was, that my mother loved. Please forgive me.

When I Awoke

Taken, he fell. I saved after him with that intent, if it was worth keeping, and inclined to sway that way.

We were two, he and I. Joined as one, a duo of synchronicity, exploring the outward bound as individuals. He brought fame and fortune in regard to the treasures of skill. Adeptitude that surpassed aptitude. Mine was a humble game; general facets of application to the tasks at hand, whatever might come our way.

We were pleasure seekers. Not the usual kind, as in ones who abhor displeasure. But ones who seek only for the examination of goodness, within the eye of discord or brilliance, both accomplishing the same aim.

He fell to his knees, and I watched him. Easy. Both the watching and the drop. Like no inhibition suspended him upward when he sought to go down. Like a stream flows without resistance, regardless of obstacle. Just over, under, above, around, another direction. Just straight while being crooked everywhere.

The Silent Partner

I wanted to catch him, but it was a faint memory of thinking I wanted something that brought a dead memory to life, where now there was only the vibrancy of the new way. The path of least resistance carved easily when the rough road left. It seemed so miraculous that it did. Then, quickly it seemed normal, like of course it should be, and always was, this way. Easy.

I watched the flow of him standing and falling, and neither held a place of preference, just the bliss that is now.

He held a grace that duller men thought only of the finest women, and they were right in sighting that, in their way.

He fell to his knees, and I cradled him in my arms with my heart, without moving. I loved him, the man who fell to his knees without limitation, with ease and surrender, and picked himself up again without an effort worthy of the scene.

For him, it was beauty, all of it, wrapped in toil of the day that would have been less succulent without. Water to lap into his breath, to make the rain contained inside, that formed with dew the innards of his abyss.

I fell for him when he fell, and I wanted the world to hear the silence.

The Place

It's late, and I am here. Lost.

I hear the cat purr. She snores in the loft above my head. The night is black. Romeo sleeps.

I wrestle with the events of the day while not caring about them at all. I envision myself walking in a free, forested, beached, rocky, flat, floating place. Other people are there. Happy people. Real happy kind of people, with real kind of happy.

We see different things, but we all know about the heartfelt stuff, the gratitude of this living and the beauty of its bread made for our creation. We smile at each other. We greet each other with easy familiarity, humour, laughter, like we all know each other, when some we have never met – well, not formally.

As I walk, I enter the forest and see the animals. It is wildly alive, as am I. The air is vibrant. I feel its breath mingle with my biology. I act silly, inside and out.

This is the place where many are, while many, many aren't. Where my real family is. I don't try to find them because I just know they are all here. I will see them when I see them, and then not, when I don't.

The forest turns into beach, and the waves come to and fro, lacking resistance, different than how it is in the wrestling place in which people are stuck. I wonder how to make those people see these sights while knowing it is impossible, without them asking to, wanting to. I feel the familiar lump in my throat of being in the place where I talk and very few understand. They are spinning, restlessly spinning. They give strangeness to a beautiful story, dull its shine. I want to scream but don't. I watch them wishing, swishing while I let go of it all.

I realise that which I cannot share loses no brilliance when kept. Deep. It never lingers without dancing, or wakes without rising. I trust without having to.

The Silent Partner

Absurd

I couldn't conquer you, even though you wanted me to. I couldn't come to your aid. I was betrayed. I couldn't lend you my ear. I was filled with fear. I couldn't bathe in your beauty. That was not my duty. I couldn't pretend to be your friend. I was your enemy. I couldn't do what you wanted me to. There was only one of me, and you were enough for two.

Two boyfriends. Two dead ends. Too many amends, at that.

The Silent Partner

I wanted a discourse from this present course, and I took one that you saw as too matter-of-fact. I didn't dare plead or beg on my knees; I was too prideless and shy for all that. But it gave me displeasure to be stuck with your measure, a voodoo doll in your pinching attack.

I didn't bear scars from prior ill regard. It was rather an unusual situation. This pounce of your prance into my life was by chance, and one of my utter disconsolation. You wanted more, for me to implore, but my nature was just as it rose. I wasn't the sort to beat a dead horse, and that got more air in your nose.

I'm sorry you're feeling a trifle misled, but I bought you a box of truffles instead, to calm your pensive petunia. You flower nicely when praised just precisely. I'd rather not fix you a bow wrapped on a package of niceties. But this I do, in spite of your hue, to brighten your colour to true blue.

I don't want to be in this comicry. I feel I have to find a way out. How do I exit without a headstand, which you'd love to see me exert? I wasn't here long, and I don't belong, even though you fancy me so. I've run out of slick, which makes this absurd, but I don't know how to leave without tricks.

I walked in the rain, and it cleared my head, though cloudy and overcast, it was. I ran into you, singing the blues, and gave you my umbrella instead.

The Silent Partner

I didn't think I'd think so much about how to end something this good. One day I'll wish that I had someone insist, but today I just want to be heard.

You looked at me like you knew I had something I wanted to say. You asked a bit politely, it seemed. Baffled I was, confused by your sincerity.

I blurted it out. I wanted to shout. Thank goodness the rain drowned my speech. I didn't find a soapbox to stand on, or we'd both have been soaked in my beseech.

I wanted to keep it shyly, to hide it from saying it outright to you. But it came out well, and I bid you farewell. It was silly, and I'll miss you in spite of me. Adieu.

Easy Street

I wanted to tell her that if she kept letting him have his way, he would. I wanted to say, "Raise a fine child and the world gets better." But my "fine" was better than most would imagine.

Pleases and thank-yous aside, it was about walking in stride with your word. It was the eye that sees the other when listening to their tales, or watches with their hearts when nothing is being said. It is acting accordingly. The idea that things are good enough, or scores are good on a sheet of made-up questions on paper, is a soulless compromise for integrity, lost in lazy times by the lesser kind. The duller mind thinks its bright idea is something new, or at least accepted as the same. How insane.

I wanted to say, "Raise the children of the world like people you want in it. Suffer now so you can suffer less. Put away the slippers and put your foot down. Hard. On the ground, like the earth that is layered upon layers and layers of fossilised change."

"But he has a strong will," she said. *To not be willed*, I thought.

Richard's Farm

After we moved to Richard's farm, I found solace in the silence of the fields and the long walks on the pasture trails. The cattle made the paths, and they ran, curvy and trodden, along the edge of the trees and next to the barbed-wire fence line. Some led to the dugout where the cows drank and where we once swam in the muddy hole amongst them. Richard later told us that the cattle wouldn't drink from there now because they could smell us in the water. All these things I never knew, never even thought of. All these things he knew about the land and the animals, which I disregarded till much later. Much, much later.

The assimilation of knowledge or some deep knowing, maybe better referred to as connection, never did forsake me. Somehow that place, the animals, the land, the gravity of its earth, its open fields and meandering cow trails, seeped into my bones and made its way into my cells. I became it, and it came with me to the mountains and everywhere else I went after I left that farm home. And all I wanted to do was leave it since I was seven years old.

I meditated in those pastures for hours, alone with the cows and grasses; sometimes so silently watching the cows eat that they came right up to my still body. I didn't move. I stared at them deeply and watchfully. I felt everything about them. They stared back, some of them, but it was the stare of a cow, an animal domesticated, humble and unsure. Yet present in the moment. Existing, by doing what it has to do in that moment. At times I watched the deer that came. At times, the deep, blank, bloated body of a dead cow being consumed by flies and maggots, peaceful and strangely violent, like a dead body in a garbage bag left to rot in your driveway, and you know it's there. Richard would hook a chain to the cow's hind legs and drag it with the tractor further into the field to let it decompose. Ugly and normal.

I did not know I was meditating till years later, when I began meditating formally. I came to see that we sometimes intuitively do things that we have not yet heard the label for. The way people label things, and then it becomes like a new thing, but it was just a natural thing you did without calling it anything.

I went out to the pastures to find the silence. Sometimes because I just wanted to get away from the awful feeling inside that I had been carrying for so long, since the last time I went into the pasture alone to be alone.

It is the feeling of holding on, enduring, trying, being in a place where one thing after another makes it hard to do any of that. Just small bits of hard ugly that make you want to cry, but you don't, and you don't know why you want to. It's just that things are so sad inside, and something important and happy is missing and will never come back. It is simply living the life you are in.

When things were awful inside the house too, I went to the pasture. Maybe after a confrontation that Richard and my mom had, or one of my siblings, if it was overly ungiving.

I ached for kindness, warmth, comfort – all of which can be called peace. Harmony. These things I built myself when I left that farm, I know now that they were melded into me by the animals of all kinds that Richard housed and I chored after and loved.

Yes, how I loved them. Bulls of mystifying nature and defiant mind, horses of all temperaments, sizes and breeds, geese and ducks and chickens of strange and eclectic disorder, cows, pigs, sheep, bees, cats, dogs, turkeys, rabbits – amazing creatures. It was a paradise of diversity, like a true Doctor Dolittle escapade.

I wanted to grow up and leave that place, its harsh words and sad measures of hurt people. Hurting people who just wanted to be understood. But it needed to fill me up with love first. Love of the earth, love of the beast, and understanding of life's burdens. And here, there, I found my silence.

The nature of the place and the torment of its daily battles led me to my inside through the outside. And here I have always been, and never left, while thinking that I was put on to that farm against my will when Mom married

Richard. That, when I left at seventeen, I was out, escaped, not going back, never looking back. And yet I took it with me – the beauty in the beast.

The Earth Roars

Back to the importance of things.
Things that are not things.
Sights that are unseen.
Words that are unspoken.
Mysteries realised.
Capsized.
Boats blundered into new shores.
Forever lands of frontiers newly discovered.
Though, familiar.

I walk the road in the new place and see my footsteps in its path. Before, I was here. Washed through sand and silt and plummeted by tides of back-and-forth relentlessness. I had forgotten, only to remember.

The outside beckons me when I am inside. This tiny earth, finite, containing as much as the little mind can bear, thinking it cannot possibly be everywhere. The inside beckons me, telling me I am free. I see outside the cosmic sphere and into the outside of the world's worlds. The lights shine so bright and pulsatingly rotate with a sight unseen.

The Silent Partner

"I am Earth and Stars and Man and Friend," it roars. Only the rumbling heart, when still, can understand. Only when its beating comes undone does it have the capacity to listen to the life which drove it, which gave it its orders, the conductor of the train. The One who rumbles beneath the noise of the earth and beyond its silence, ever present.

I see the motion stop, the outward motion. Sleeping feet stop their restless beat, and woes explode into never-never land with stillness overtaking their frontier. I see it go, all of it. The fragility of the mind and its weak links to nothingness that is, simply, ether.

Then the real blast booms, the unrelenting call to home, the drone of magnitude in sound so earthy this is indeed what it creates. No mistake.

But in its essence, as I linger, I find finer the hidden door from where comes the roar. As I enter it, there is no more sound, only mystical lights of silent beauty shining in unison where the many become the One.

The Silent Partner

Hazy Affection

Why do I even care about what makes you tick? It's like waiting for a time bomb. Exasperating. Wondering if it is going to go off, and strangely, sickeningly thinking it's kind of exciting if it does, and yet being relieved when it doesn't.

We're a strange lot. Nervous wrecks. Wrecking balls. Destroying the beauty of us to get a shred of excitement, however shredded it gets.

We want it all – peace, love and rock 'n' roll oblivion. The dominion of our contrived lives coming loose so we can finally lose control over what we never had under our thumb anyway.

Hazy days. Spent looking for a speck of crumb that we can paste into our glitter ball. That is all. Waiting for it to explode and not wanting it to, over and over and over again and again and again.

I wanted to befriend you, but you were a loose cannon and I was a yogi. What do you suppose would happen? You'd explode in meagre meanderings, and all I'd want was meaning in deeper things – and to see you standing there, while I watched you in this dream from far away. You'd say I was disconnected, but I was only distanced from your hypocrisy trying to capture me and reel me into your drama scene. You're a queen. Or anything else you'd like to be. The acting is free for the taking.

I'm not mistaken. Just exploring. I wait for the door to open while gently pushing against it, daily, constantly knocking gently, pounding, to hear the sounding of the rip-roaring waves on the door's other shore calling more to me than you do. I feel so close that I get damp, chilled from the spray. I take it away. Another step closer to seeing the spree come to life inside me, setting me free to be alive, to live somewhere else inside my mind, to be ruled by my heart and the White Ruler of Justice who beckons inside me, leading me on to where I know I belong.

It's my only addiction. I can't compete with you. It's my one and only addiction, an affliction of sorts. Wanting to set another course, the one that returns me up the highway, taking me north while birds fly south to winter. I want to climb instead. North, from my toes to my head. In a freezing rain, against the grain of most, where I can feel the cool breeze send shivers up my spine. Where I can come alive inside.

God hides in the mountains, the tops of them. You must climb to find him there, to reach him. He makes his bed there, at the top of the top.

I want to feel the spin of him. Shake the nonsense out of me and spin me into ecstasy. I want to land dizzy, to jump off the merry-go-round while it's still spinning low below. Off I go.

It's my only addiction, my affliction. The distancing of myself to follow the distant drummer to his beat, to read the smoke signals till I see the flame in my eye. To burn with knowing, and to warm the icy journey to my soul with blazon bravos that speaks to me of ecstasy gone away from the usual frivolity.

Still, I dream of you and you don't know, as only a dream apparition would. Pretending to be something more on the surface, but lacking the stride of one who has something inside. Some guts deserving of glory.

Hazed, you tease the world, to believe it is real. To believe it is something that needs attention for longer than a simple encounter of amusement. You excuse yourself for pretending so. You're not serious. It's not serious or sensical. Only temporary. Fleeting away.

I'm not on drugs. Not a dope. I know there's no coping needed to bend a dream to reality when it's only there for my amusement. Till I find the door to the ocean that washes it all away.

Sleep, my child. Life stands at your demand for you to understand its power lies solely within your hands. Strike your affection with wisdom. Then land it and never look back at the dream, exception being the love from which it was created to get you outside of it.

Engineer the mountain. Bestow the gift of tsunami upon the watershed of the world, and restore the power of mastery to your creating hands.

The Steed

Be still. The dying steed so quick to leap. To bolt. The strength of your stamina is in the silence of still grass and meadows undisturbed.

I come to the pasture to feed and to feast on the simple pleasure of life. The food as my fodder is the milk of my mother. The rays of her warmth, the sunshine that gleamed her coat, and the red blood that ran through her veins, locked in carvings of venous delight. All this came from above into the ground, and through the grass below her feet, which she did eat.

I feel the wind willow-whip through my mane, and I am not moved by its course, its direction. I am the same. I am held to stand. Tall.

The pleasures of my meadow go uninterrupted by the beauty of the day, the unpleasantries of the same. I still remain.

What would you have me do? Move? Race through the trails to take the lead? Saunter through the valley and climb steep hills? I am the steed.

The Silent Partner

Or stay? For a while or till all journeys' end? Long or arduous, I care not of its length or endurance. In the end, I am the same steed, only weathered some. Temporarily.

Pin labels upon my back and stroke my side with adorned ribbons, stabled warmly with good feed. It matters not the consequence or action of my deeds.

I am the same. I remain. I am the Noble Steed.

Hosting Colour

I draw the outline of you and let the grey fill in the rest where you want to smile, to tweak your brow, to notice something interesting.

I weave the colours of your face, shades of grey, patches of pink, some more black, some more red, some yellow, some white. The days before, even the score of what you are filled in with today. What colour are you, the tangled hues of years gone by that affected you?

There is a rainbow lit inside your head that arches to the centre of your being. Your downward spiral in life, uplifted by fixation on the betterment of you, who could be king. I strike the strands of the arc, and unlike a child's flimsy bow, these glow in colours interpreted to utmost, infinite direction when given attention, their paint long hanging fresh in its vibrancy of light. You would have wished you could have seen this earlier, but now you are only grateful. You spin within, prisms releasing prisons.

I try to hide what I found inside and, for the most, it goes even when it glows so. Some just say, "You're happy today," and never track the knowing. Some give a curious slant, that upward brow, to wonder how you're so. Then think so smugly that they know. They don't.

You form the shell that binds you to overflowing. Soon you will need a bigger home to bear your goods, even though all you pack is you. You have no baggage, only your big heart and your rainbow, beaming.

The grey you are begins to fade. It gets stacked with black and erased till white appears. You become defined not in contradiction, but rather in direction. You no longer are a mere outline. You represent a line. And then you fill your shell with blues and greens, yellows and reds, and you are illuminated instead.

I want to cry with passion as I draw the colour in you. But I subdue. One more complete to go. How I love you so. All round and found you have become.

I wish to draw more like this one.

The Silent Partner

Oar

To the boat I swam. Drowning – I was drowning. Gulps and gasps of that precious air filled me, and I spat the water out. The water of my soul, its heavy weight filling my lungs. I wanted it to. I wanted it to.

Scared, I swam to the boat to get to the shore. I wonder where the glory is in all this. The make-believe glory of heroes passing time, looking for crusades. I was self-made. From putty formed into hardened rock, but clay still the same. The water melted me away, showing what I was made of. Weakness. Sand that had nothing to cling to but its own grains, which slipped away with each grasp and grab. Nothing firm. No substance. No sustenance.

Who put me here on this boat afloat to nowhere? I wanted it back. The air I breathed when life was lighter, ballooning into good times and party scenes.

You told me I was no good, no longer you.

I didn't care, or so it seemed, the days of long ago locked in between my crevices of blank stare back at you. I took it in. Like silk, what you said slithered into my eyes and

The Silent Partner

made its way down my throat, forming a lump there for a while. A short while. Till I swallowed it down hard, but without outside effort so you wouldn't notice. It went down and slunk into the crevices of me, filling them, till it landed in my heart. And there it sat, folded nicely for safekeeping. Folded and blank. Blank blue, so very blue. The blanket of what you said, as it sat inside me covering my heart and filling my gut.

I said nothing. Maybe something short and too calm like, "Okay, have it your way" or, "You need to do whatever it is you need to do." But inside I sank, like the heavy blue blanket I swallowed with your leaving. It was getting weighted, heavy from the weight of your words. Wetter, with its drowning.

I went to the water to swim when you left. I smiled a courteous goodbye, and I could see you seemed sad in return, but I caught a glimpse of skip in your step as you started to approach what took you further away from me, from us.

I waddled to the water now, carrying my anchor that was you, and us, now put afloat. I put it in the boat. But the shimmer beneath, when I rowed to the deep, was so appealing it caught my eye. I wanted to die. To dive right in and see what was lurking inside these still, dark waters. What life was there amongst the waves that rocked this boat and yet kept it afloat? Was it different? Lighter than it seemed, and lighter than I remember? I seemed lighter now, like pure delight. I felt so heavy right now. Something must be less than this, lighter than this, something that mattered more than this weight, something I could float to, with my wet blanket soaked inside of me.

I stared into the dark abyss, crooked my head to see the depth of the water there. I was so sure I saw something unique in the deep. It looked like grief, but the welcoming kind, the one that was better than mine. I told myself to go closer, strain further, bend nearer, so the front of my torso could lean forward, so I could lay the blame into the top of me, lifting it up from deep below. Till over it goes.

There and then, I went into the water. Not forcibly or eagerly, just silkily. My blanket unravelling its fold into the dark, deep wet. I started to sink. I drank it in. That floating feeling, going down. It felt good. I was so thirsty. I drank and drank and gulped the gallons. They were like the good water after the drunk of the night before with its galore.

I didn't love her. The thought came to me.

"What?" I said, to my head.

I didn't love her.

"Why are you here, then, taking up the dead? Besides, love is better when alive. You stupid thing. Don't you know anything?"

The Silent Partner

I coughed the first cough that turned into gasps and groans from filled water canals where sweet air used to float. The stuff that dreams were made of. Are made of.

"Aaaeee!" I screamed in between the thoughts of death that raced through my head. "Aaaeee! Over a woman, you fool! You're so uncool!"

I saw the boat.

There's always a life preserver in your time of need. Just look for it. And breathe.

The Silent Partner

The Black Panther

I didn't see him there, though he watched me all along. I thought I was alone, more alone than words can say.

He cradled me when I was young, and then I went it alone. On the dusty road of life, I got dirtied up.

It took years of discovery to figure out the truth. Late nights, failed friends, fancy dances and fatherless days. I didn't care for what I thought I didn't know about. I wasn't scared to death about the things I didn't remember. Daddy's death.

I toddled to and fro, in high-topped baby shoes. White and leathery, laced with cord like the olden days. Some say early memories start at preschool, but I recall the weightlessness of my unsteady frame as a toddler. Toddling in these white shoes, polished with white polish from a tube that had a foam top. Squirt. Out came the polish. Squirt. That's what they called me. Small and all.

The panther stalked my mind and crawled into my soul when I was there late at night in the dark. That's when the panther comes. No one ever said the panther stalks but is afraid just the same. But be serious. He sees the demons in the beauty of the night. The threshold of doors to distant places that are invisible to the naked eye in the daylight hours. He knows where those demons go. Nowhere.

I felt him crawl inside of me and stay there. He brought me faith and bravery, and fear within his fearsomeness.

From then on, he and I were one. He was gifted to me from misery, the death of my dad. The father I wanted to have.

I stalked the streets and walked the valleys in the dusk to join the creatures in their place. I sighed inside from the aliveness I felt in their land. I tingled with excitement, on the edge of what was moving when most would think it was simply standing still. But I could feel. The vibration, toddling back and forth, to and fro in the slightest movement, so rapidly it felt like breathlessness.

It was missing. All the other parts. The reason why; the repeated starts. Of new things that were old, getting past the last thing till the next thing. It came to head. Daddy's dead.

I saw the links clink, in soft demure like a baby's blanket, the gentle ones that were thin with cosy diapered edges that would wrap you so tight you knew you could hold on with all your might, and life was good. You thought you understood. You were swaddled by arms that came from a place where sinew was made from spades and kindness, and these things were never dropped. Safety, it was. Hanging on to something with all your innocence.

I left a stare standing there in my fully pink painted dress. A band in my hair that was hardly there, the baby kind. I didn't know then what I would pretend for the rest of my days. Till today. Daddy's dead now, and you're all alone. God took him. He's with him to stay.

The blackness inside, from the panther I am, filled me with deepness within. The tan of the hide, silk and shiny and black, gave me a very tough skin. The agility of his leap, I took as my own because we were one and the same. I took the leaps of faith every day, in big ways. It was the only way for me to be him.

The words came through, so long repressed. Stressed. Fifty years they've been laid to rest. The world was toddling, tipped off its kilter. Tilted. Daddy's dead. Daddy's dead. Daddy's dead. Everything is a mess.

Reaching Riches

The saga of "so far away" continues to plague the earth. Everything's so far away. Everything I'm trying to reach, always trying to reach for something that seems out of reach.

I'm not rich enough to reach. Rich with admiration for faraway places with generous wings floating everything. I still think I need silver platters that clatter with splatter. I still want bang and boom when I enter a room. Big shot. Party hog. Hair of the dog.

I've spent my night's worth on false frankincense and myrrh, and I still expect to be rich in the morning. The morning after the *duldry*, the doldrums of adultery. Mixed-up, messy-headed, barely alive, so I must be deadish.

I don't want to know me anymore, but I don't have a choice. We're stuck together, aren't we? Weren't we? Ugh. Too sluggish to hang around with you acting like a zoo, the strange animal that comes to roost and then boasts like she knows. Egad, it's so sad. How do I get rid of you, or make us sane?

Can I do it while playing your game? You'd think me a fool then, and accuse me of ridicule, even though the irony of that puts me in stitches. You are too big for your britches while walking around town with your pants hanging down.

A sloth that has endless energy for frivolity. I want you away from me. I want to be depleted from your energy, which saps the life out of me and leaves me hanging there, loaded for bear that never comes.

Leave me alone, won't you? But no, no, we're stuck together. How do I get loose from you?

I hear the slap of water against a shore. A chain gang sloshing through, banged together with iron feet and clad hands. I want to be with them, to be free to have some direction.

Clank. Clank. Clank.

Hanging on a thread of desire, thinking the sinners are free because they're paying their fines for their crimes, and I haven't yet saddled up to repent mine.

What grips you to me, like misery that loves company? The comfortable smell of home cooking fried to a crisp, till you can't tell what it is, but you think you know it just the same.

I'm sick and tired of playing this game of winner and loser where no one ever wins, just screeches when reaching another shore, just like the one they've landed on before. The empty dime all the time. Time spent, no repent. I've spent enough on you.

The Last Hallway

When I saw the door open, I went in.

Romeo says, "When the light is green, go."

It's dark. A hallway turned into a tunnel of holy cow. Stunning. Batman would love this. Holy cow, Batman! Striking – not just the space, but the sound that it resonates. Tolling as a bell in a tower. Sideways. The tower is sideways like a hallway. This hallway.

I run to the side and stay. It reminds me of home. The way, anyways. It is dark and dense and comfortingly cold. Crisp, with its sensation of icicles in the air, frozen droplets playing.

Romeo would say go, but he wouldn't go.

My head pounds from the force of the state that wants to come within, and I cringe and grin. It doesn't mock me or stop me. I know its patience and mine, all a matter of time.

Changing it, rearranging it, forcing it through the illusion of obstacle, like pretending the light is going to change. To yellow. To slow. To caution. No, the eyes betray the truth of reflection.

My heart hurts, not aching, but a systematic prolonging non-desire to get nowhere, but the simple expansion of this moment into the breaking of the hallway walls. It nudges me from inside to say there is nothing to be done with this nudging till the door opens into the window of my mind, locked deep inside. I don't want to wait. I don't want to hurry. The in-between is like a squeezing with no pressure.

Someone turns the light on. Someone bright that no one, but the very few, notice. Like the dragonfly that flitters, and you barely hear its wings, but you do if you're the type who might notice. The prepared one. The flutter, faint. So faint you hear it after the fact. Then you've lost sight of its flight. Rather, the moment, the exact moment of its suspension, when it begged to get your attention. You were supposed to notice, to go. The light is green. The door is open. Flutter. There's no in-between with green. You look as you hear the flutter after the fact, and there's nothing there except perhaps remnants of what was. You tell yourself you saw it, and you did, but you didn't while you did.

I hear the train in the Dragon Fly's roaring wings. The rumble as it approaches is loud and long.

I say I must first finish my task at hand, and then I will look at you. There's time. The moment lasts forever. The light it emits with fluttering wings is brilliant, delight. I am blinded with blues and greens and in-betweens.

Go. The light is green. The wings flutter so loudly I can smell them. The air moves its biology into ecology.

The Dragon Fly is in the hallway. It starts down it, though the beginning is always beginning. It has never started, and it is always new. My friend nudges me, and I see. Friends in high places. There are more. More dragons flying. Some with long tales, hidden in dens amongst the hallway, some breathing out fire from a long sleep, with jagged tails and stories of the same. Tales of crooked dimension, rocky, whippy, cragged and crazy, hazy and dark, then burned bright with fire, flame upon flame. Smokin' clear.

I step again. The hallway is lit with it. Thousands of thousands of breaths, of beatings, of hearts, of wings, of fluttering moments lit by shining wings of crystal prisms. There is colour, all of it. Green. Go. Step further. No, again. To the same and different.

I smile. The hallway lights, and the door swings like a saloon bar entry. *Come inside*, it beckons. *Come inside from the outside*. Which is which? The far side of the hallway is now near in sight. I jump.

The hole is deep and steep. Steeeep. I love the feeling without caring. My house is being cleaned, swept by dragon wings, while roaring trains clear out its debris, strewing it below, somewhere low.

Bothersome

I didn't circle you. As you lay dead, face down on the pavement, I couldn't find any chalk. I chalked it up to the fact that maybe you didn't need to be circled.

You waited around for me, in history. Always lingering, some would say loitering. I think you were actually accused of that in my apartment building, when you were hanging around, waiting to see if you could sneak in the security door when no one answered your buzzer. My buzzer, the buzzer you were buzzing.

Let go of me. Finally. If I wanted you there, you'd know I cared. But it's just me being nice 'cause I don't know what else to do to get rid of you.

Maybe I'd miss you, when you were gone. If you ever left. Maybe I'd hang my head and cry as if you'd died. Perhaps I'd feel so bad inside. Sad, for the things we didn't do when I didn't want to be with you any longer.

It's been a long time – well, only days, but long ones since you left. You walked in the park, they said, and there they found you. Dead. Well, fallen down from your throne, anyways, your crown bouncing on the pavement. Nothing gushed out. You were still in a pout, being silent for no reason. Well, a mad one, maybe. You are such a baby.

I tiptoed over to see the commotion in the park. The onlookers looking, some of them touching you, nudging you with their shoe as if to wake you without wanting to wake you, just in case you were a crazy person. They must know you well. My crazy person. You give off that aroma, I think. The kind that makes you think you don't stink when you bother people. People like me.

I knew you were waiting for me, so I would come and see you in the park. The travesty you'd made for yourself to blow things out of proportion. It wouldn't get a reaction. I'm sold out of stories about you. They came so cheap and plentiful, it was easy to get rid of them all.

Now what should I do? Stand here and stare at you with the rest of the crowd that doesn't know what's under your skin, toe-tapping you to get you to stop making a spectacle, while awkwardly wondering if there is something there. Something they should care about 'cause you're lying here, dead, in the park on the pavement.

They look around for someone who knows you, might know you, to take you off their hands. I wish the same for me. Why won't you go away to somewhere else, someplace that has something for you, other than this basket case you've climbed into?

The Silent Partner

I find some chalk and draw your form around you. One crazy leg, the second one; one annoying arm, two. One head so full of yourself. I make it larger to capture all your nonsense that's trying to burst out. Then I flip you over. I hear oohs and aahs as you go. I colour your nose with the blood on your face. Now you look like the clown you are. People stare. You grin, to my chagrin, and I wish I could bolt out of here.

A Musk Deer

Cheatin' heart. Wanting what it doesn't have. Honour. Veracity. Beauty in the big state.

I wonder how you will ever figure out that the wife you have is the one you need. Greedy you. Walking and talking the blues, wanting green. The colour of money, the grass is always greener kind.

I don't mind. I watch you leave for bigger things, and I feel space. I pace in it. Pace myself to enjoy the freedom, the fifteen minutes you go to the store and I don't see you, feeling like I don't need you anymore. The hour you retreat to the den, to spin your roulette wheel on banking business, sports figures or boring news, all crying your blues. Every minute you look for a clue that isn't you, and you latch on to it like a carnivore. You're a vegetarian, you know. You don't know.

You grow yourself from seeds and spurts of tiny gems planted in your behind-the-scenes saga, the one you don't notice. The passers-by glance – not in a woman's trance, but the musk deer on the side of the road looking at you through the window of your sports car. You're too *stuped-*

up to see. You grow a nose for smelling out bad company, while the wildflowers on the side of the road blow their scent so strikingly in your direction to get your attention, so you would know the aroma of intoxicating bliss doesn't come from a perfume bottle. They want you to know. But you don't know.

You grow two hands to help the man sitting hunched on the side of the road, tying his shoe. You think he's worn out, but you don't know he's a worn-out version of you. He extends his hand weakly as you race by, flying to your next due date; brew date with a friend who won't wait if you're late. He has endless time now, this old guy. Time to feel the impact of the shuffle of his feet on the city street. His life is less fleeting, while only waiting for a kind passer-by to smile and say hi.

You cover your ears against the wind whistling through and turn loud the pound of the sound of today's latest tune or yesterday's news. It reminds you of you. Your baby cries as your wife rocks it to sleep, but you're out on the town, peeping around. It doesn't matter. You don't know, and you tell yourself so. She doesn't miss you, your hugs and your kisses, your caring ways and sweet embrace, replaced by the new love in her arms that she wants to make into something true. Something from you.

They say love is blind. They don't know.

The Silent Partner

Eskew

From the centre, it sprang at me. I backed away and went in again. It took a while till it sprang again. I thought it wouldn't. I thought it might not. I started to relax, to believe what I wanted to believe: that I was right. I even smiled a little, waiting. To smile a lot. To gloat while appearing modest, and yet thankful. Pretty darn thankful.

But it took me by surprise the second time. I had to admit it. Hated to admit it. The second time I was totally caught off guard. Even when I knew it was coming, saw it coming. And I had been bit before. Pretty hard. Not scarred, but deep enough.

I wished I wasn't here to have to witness me. What was I to do? I had to cross this. This cross I was carrying. Or it would come to my grave with me. Grave, it was. Serious. Even though no one would ever notice. Except me, witnessing me. I hated myself. The gullible guy, the gallant girl. The sad one.

I wanted to cry, but that made me the girl and not the man I wanted to be. I'm sick of me.

Slippery I became. Sleek and sly, except inside where I was crying like a baby suckling. All I wanted was a bonnet to hang my head into. Pink or blue, it didn't matter. I just wanted the string to be on it, to tie tightly around my neck. Maybe in a bow.

Silently I crept into me, while I put on a smile to others. I thought they deserved it. They were trying too. They were washing themselves clean every day. Showering, bathing, trying to get clean. I couldn't fault them for what they didn't know. I didn't know either. Ignorant, we walked together. We talked and laughed and shared a bit of what we wanted to, dared to. In moments of weakness, we shared more stories of us. Letting a bit of the letting-go part of us out, the sacred, scared part. Just enough to be funny, maybe a bit interesting, but not too much to make it weird. Where someone smiled but then didn't see you for a while because you crept too much into what we didn't talk about. Because you touched their hidden web, and they were scared they too might let their spider out. Sometimes they just bit back in this way. Silence. Stalking, it was. Waiting for you to get too close to the centre, and then scrambling out it came, like hysteria with direction, firm and protective. Fangs to sink into you. But all you saw was the mouth. The teeth were hidden in your skin.

You hoped you didn't cross the line. That you provided just enough to be unique without being termed a geek. It would be hard to live that one down. You might even have to move to another town, or find other ways to get around

The Silent Partner

so you couldn't run into those who tagged you as a freak anymore. Weirdo.

How softly you needed to come out. How watchfully you needed to observe. How centred you needed to be while seeming aloof, casual, transfixed. Bewitched.

I developed a twitch. It helped. It showed what was happening on the inside a little more. For some reason, others related to me better. My line was being jerked just a bit, and it made me seem like a good catch, like I was more honest, more real than the rest. But it was just the knot in my web that was pulling at my heart, trying to pull me apart, bit by bit. The centre of you. In eschew. Gone askew. *Eskew*.

Pardon Me, But I Love You

Playfulness came. I wasn't at the playground or in town or hanging around. I was doing my thing. The thing I always do. Watching life come through.

It came.

Like a subtle play on words that you kinda miss and then grin, when you realise, and keep remembering it. Remembering how you missed it, but yet not really. How it caught you gently by surprise, yet you felt like you caught it.

Like summer rain. Small drops that lead to a downpour when you don't care if you get wet because it's warm. You're warm inside and out. Warm and comfortable, but okay for anything to happen, 'cause nothing could disrupt this, only add to its embracing, its fuzzy, hugging feeling.

Like smiling when your lips are soft and supple, and it comes so easy you don't even notice, but you do, 'cause you know you're the one doing it. You like it, smiling subtly. And the grin that breaks, too. The one that is suddenly the laughter out loud breaking the smiling into big.

It feels playful, but more so. Playfulness.

Like a flowing dress. Like tree-strewn branches you're hauling in the woods to build your sky-high fort into, to camouflage it. To say you're not a man today but a joyous boy or wispy girl, floating and flying. Anywhere.

You act stern sometimes; as part of your duty, you feel you need to. But the kidney shape of your gut is smiling upwards. You feel lucky. Invincible. In a soft, playful kind of way. Like nothing could ruin the day.

You hear things. Sounds. The ones that are really there. Drums in the distance. Crunch of your feet on the earth. Birds talking – not squawking, but talking in a language you're sure you understand. You hear words that make you know, and you're pleasantly surprised as it passes through you. Breezingly.

Will you come and play with me today? I have a castle near here. Well, up the way. It's between the pines and is a bit of a climb. It's guarded by some friends of mine. They're making a beat out of pounding sticks and doing childlike things, and they'd love for you to stay. As long as you can till you need to go away. Again.

The Silent Partner

The Donkey

It's hidden for a reason. I can't find it. There are so many clues. I keep following them. Warmer, warmer, warmer, getting hot, almost there. Cold. Dead again. Starting from the beginning. But yet not able to let go of what I thought I saw before. The clues that took me warmer to the hot spot, the bright light. The end of the game.

Were those clues right? Was I on the right track? Or were they red herrings, erring me to never-never land, behind door number three? Where the donkey stands waiting for me to ride it off the stage. Stubborn, I am.

I think it gets a bad rap, the donkey. I'm not trying to talk myself into why the donkey's not such a bad prize after all. How losers tell you they didn't really want to win anyways 'cause they're happy with their meagre prize. Likening their like of lack. I just think maybe the donkey could be a great prize. Riding out on it, the burro carrying my burdens. The greatest burden being me. At least I wouldn't have to carry me all by myself anymore.

I'll admit it. I want the big prize. Okay, I've said it. The big one. The larger-than-life one. The one that you can't win.

The Silent Partner

The one you have to earn by following the clues in the game, till – bingo!

I put my marks on my bingo card one by one, as the matching numbers are called. I need only B3 to win this game, to call bingo. G49 is said instead. This game is dead. I pull a new bingo card and begin again. One by one, the numbers are drawn and called out. When they call B3, I think, *It's me!* I'm back at that old stack. Glancing at that old door. Playing that old game. Wondering if I could have won somehow. I have to turn the pile upside down so I can't see the stack from the past anymore. To concentrate on this new play.

I've missed a few of the numbers now. They keep coming though, no end in sight. They lead me to somewhere.

A place to hang my hat for a while.

Something of Substance

Head to toe into the dungeon. He pushed me. The palm of his hand on the back of my neck. Against my neck. Me, straining, resisting. It was like a neck brace, choking me. My feet followed. I wasn't leading them. They were being pushed and trailing behind like they had no choice. They didn't. The time for choosing was over. I was being held here. Pushed. Against my will.

This place was dark and damp and rank. It smelled like the dungeon it was. A place for creepy things, spiders and things, which were the least of my worries. I worried now. What would the morning bring? The one where the sun doesn't come up inside this cell? This jail. The sun doesn't shine in hell.

The dark days would rise now. How would I be able to fill my time, the rest of my days, just staring off into space in the dark damp of this dungeon? Where would I find the stars to twinkle in this black, to light my way and tell me everything was okay? How would I know that whatever I did, the light would still come round, would still rise on the horizon, that beautiful sun? The one I took for granted on days unlike today.

I wanted to go back to what I knew. I wanted to cry for my mother. I wanted to revisit all the missed visits, the flowerless Mother's Days, and the times I didn't care about anyone but me. I wanted to be caring, like I wasn't when I was free, to choose.

Locked in this castaway place, I wanted grace. How to be the beggar when I had been the fool? I told myself life was cruel to me, while I never cared to realise my own cruelty.

There was a scratching in the dark after the heavy door boomed closed and the clink of the key left me here, locked inside this dungeon for evermore.

There was a scratching, after a while. I don't know how long it had been. Maybe days or weeks or months or years, all compiled of endless hours. I wasn't sure where it came from at first. I had been so accustomed to the stench, the rank; I didn't think about sound amongst the silence. I thought it didn't exist, that lost sense, the voices in my head being the exception.

They stayed on, yearning, accusing, telling me my story with the blues. They told me tales of things I'd seen, stopping in the middle, so I wouldn't be able to open the door without the key. They mimicked me. Told me a sorrowful tale, and just before it came to the happy ending, they threw away the glee to leave me slumped in misery. They left it hanging in the scary air, out of reach, hoping I'd lose my mind in the waiting, in the craving.

I came to the conviction that I couldn't, wouldn't listen to them anymore. I didn't need the company of these awful, spiteful folks inside of me. Who were they, anyways – these voices in my head, taunting me, convincing me I was better off dead? I lost touch with them on purpose. It was worth it. The games they played were such a charade; I was left in agony, trying to stop their vicious play on me. So in the silence I stayed. It lasted so long I thought all the sound was gone. I thought it never existed.

Until the scratching. The attack of the rat upon my back. It came in nibbles at first. Tiny bites, gnawing. Titbits of snippets of razor-sharp teeth, picking at my spine through the hole in my neck it was digging itself into. Tick, tick, tick. The rhythm of it. Grooving. It was nice to be touched, wanted, enjoyed. The sound was musical, music to my ears, but he hadn't gotten to them yet. He was still at my neck.

I waited a bit, feeling his nudging under my hair as something worth wearing, only to be touched. Soothed. Tasted and touched. To be thought savoury, even by a beast, was comforting.

He chewed on me some. It hurt like glass cutting slivers into me. Perhaps like those who see a shard and marvel at it as they cut their outsides open. Like freedom, the chaotic kind, the great escape into the place you want to escape from once you arrive.

The Silent Partner

Hell-bent, it was. This place. This dungeon. The insanity of my mind. The rat on my back. The love of his attack. I was losing it. And I didn't care, for once.

It was different, not caring. I was pretty caring for my pretty self. Always thinking about how to get what I wanted. Always thinking about how to be the best man for me. How to be free in the moment, wrapping myself in wanting. Wanting to fill myself with anything that satisfied my cravings.

I wanted a drink, the kind with substance. It led me to wanting more substance – the stuff that ended in abuse. The substance abuse that never had any substance after all. That kept leading me nowhere, except here. It led me here. The substance that got me to give up liberty by taking liberties with others' property. Others' personage. That got me to steal to get more substance that evaporated in me, after getting me higher, to take me lower into depths that kept me looking for more.

I thought the common man was a joke. Walking around like a folk tale, working here and there, bringing his purse home to feed simple mouths with simple things. I thought I was keener. I wanted the greener grass, the pleasure pastures of relaxation, that took me flying high in my mind with inspiration; that never went anywhere, but landed me sweating on the dirty floor in the morning, wanting more.

How would I get my next kick, so I could rise again without using my own two feet, or my head? I'd given up thinking of ways to get beyond that included my community. I was outside of society. That wasn't for me. I was on the free ride, getting high. My toll was paid to get this way by the bills I'd laid in the palm of the hand of the man on the corner. The dark hallway into the alley, where shady ways get played. I was gay when I was up. Not homosexual, but happy – though I was okay either way. The ups and downs were worth it to me. I'd sold my body to any who looked longingly at me. I'd have sold my soul too. But it left when I did, taking flight to higher places, while I took my high that spiralled me downwards as the gas of substance ran out. I was a fool messing with freedom that I thought came easily. Cheap and easy. Until the rat on my back reminded me that I was easily taken and no one cared for me, but me.

I reached gingerly with my fingers to the back of my neck. I could hear it loudly now. The gnawing. I wanted to touch it. I felt its breath. The smell of a rat, intact. It sniffed at me. Its whiskers flickered on my fingers as I reached behind me tenderly. My mind flashbacked to the cat I'd had when I was young, licking my fingers after I finished my dinner plate. My mother smiling at me.

The food on this platter today was me. I was the fodder for a rat in a cell, eating its last meal in jail.

Catering

I saw you standing in the doorway. We smiled a wicked smile. How were we going to serve this many people and get out of here alive? Smiling. I was glad you were in this with me. This thing we'd gotten ourselves into. Our latest gig.

"Yes, sir," I said. "Happy to help, sir. Let me top that up for you, sir. Let me see if I can find some in the kitchen. Uh-huh. Yes, I will." I nodded my head.

The famous line "Let me check" got me out of there for a while. Even though I *was* going to check. I could let my breath out in the kitchen and gaze outside at the patio deck that I'd be walking upon in about five hours.

The youth of youth was still sticking in me. I didn't even think about that; it just was there. Tired only from the long day and repetition, but as soon as this scene changed, my insides would be bright again with mojo. Yahoo.

We didn't have anything planned, just hanging out. Walking home, playing cards, burning candles, chatting in the dim light about life. Friends' time. No purpose but that. Figuring things out together, little by little, discussing life's scenarios, and then just letting it go as the candle flame flickered.

I'd make you a cup of tea, or we'd sip a pop, snack snacks, and have a game of cribbage. No one cared who won; we'd been on both sides so many times. I'd let you; you'd let me bend the rules. No matter if a card was played, you could change your mind. This was life, and a woman's prerogative, anyways.

You'd stay late, and then I'd see you to the door, and you'd walk home. It was easy, the way we were. Back and forth, equal ease. See-saw. Sometimes more weight on my side, but we knew it went the other way eventually, soon. And we were just so good with that, we never even thought about, let alone talked about it.

The notion came to me one day to do something extra. I sprang you a hearty party with all the fixings. You roamed in with ease, so used to that scene, and started picking up platters and handing out napkins. I swear I saw you with my apron on, tied backwards like you like.

When you served me my potion of choice, I laughed out loud inside and said, "Well, thank you, ma'am."

It was your party, after all, and now I was the belle of the ball. It didn't matter. We knew all the time. The way to a good heart is through another.

Clueless

Putting on the ritz, playing along like a broken record. Not broken, just scratched in patches. But you'd wash yourself clean and buff yourself up so nobody would notice. Like the shower after the hangover. Going to your parents' house for dinner the day after you've been bingeing like a dancing queen, drama scene the night before. That is, if your parents are decent folk and not the kind that might have raised someone like you. Clueless.

It's fun, the way of the world. Wayward and all. Till the great fall. The one you inevitably take. And then bang your head, but not hard enough, because you just keep getting up.

You need to stay there for a while. Down low, looking at your toes. Dissecting every inch of you to see what's in between those cracks and slivers, that slither when you walk, when you're up and about. Strutting. Putting on the ritz.

I watched you your whole life. Not all of mine. I saw you before you were you, the thought of you planted in someone's heart, where you got your start. Bang! You came out with a bang. Almost landed on the floor, you were so slippery. But you didn't. Someone caught you that time. You'd make up for it on your own, though, later. And you'd like it that way. Landing on the floor. Playing it up like a baboon's perfume, scented awkwardly, erotically and awfully. Big lips. Swinging hips. Swaying to and fro, like a monkey so. Doing its business like monkeys do.

You were that, a little monkey, when you were little. Climbing everywhere. Dancing on chairs. Your parents hollered, "Get down from there!" But you were up. And then fell down. The dent in your crown of glory. Gory it was, to watch you fall.

I got used to it. The arm's-length glance watching you, without any obligation to do, to change you into anything except another party dress you were trying to squeeze yourself into.

I bided my time and held my breath. Not waiting, but in calm anticipation. It was inevitable, eventual. You would fall again. Would you stay down? When would you examine it closely? Those clothes, that mud on your nose, that dose of poses that didn't smell anything like roses. Baboon.

I called you that. It stuck, like everything else did to you. Sticky, candied you, covered in syrup, coated in taffy. Tacky baboon. That's you. Little one who never grew up. I'm tired of watching you fall.

The Silent Partner

I close my eyes. I don't look at you. No more watching you. You are a bad dream born of thought, clothed in flame. Flamboyant you.

I want to slam the door. Not to offend you, but so that I will know it is locked tight. So there's no mistake that it has mistaken you for someone else and let you in.

I hope you grow. I hope for repose. For your positioning into something less cushioning than your padded life. The interference it plays, not letting you fall down. Hard. Not to hurt you. Just to land you. Solidly, somewhere on the earth, so you'd be birthed into someone new. Someone who's not so clueless. Someone glued to the inner tube on the wheel of life.

Somehow I'd like to see you implode. Get hold of yourself and have to hold it together for a while – a long while. All by yourself, till your arms get tired, till you get so weary of holding yourself together that you begin to realise how the rest of us feel. And you learn appreciation for how mistaken you've been.

Higher Ground

I didn't rise above it all. Not all of it. But a good portion. Enough to get my foot in the door. The new door. The one where all of this crap that I needed to get beyond wasn't going. It couldn't follow me. And I tried to not step on its scree as I was making my way out. Up and out. Outta here, over there. When I say over, I mean over. Over the top of the trash. Over it. Beyond the rubbish, the garbage that needs to be recycled to get on a new programme. I hope it goes. All of it. I hope it all goes, and I hope it all goes well. Goodbye, trash pile.

I smile – the grin of "finally". The grin that I had hoped would come. The upward turn of my lips, both of them together going high. Beyond the frown I used to wear but tried not to. I got caught up in it. Rather, down. I got caught down, in its downward pull. Even my step dragged, sagged, my pants bagged. Haggard, I was, ragged from the gravity that was keeping me down. Thank God for the earth that stopped my descent. I would have been pulled right through by my nose, bulldozed into the ground beneath me. Nose first into the dirt, 'cause I just kept smelling trouble.

The Silent Partner

Smelling the stale air and wondering where it came from. Years passed. I still sniffed that gas. Searchingly. It led me to me with my nose in a pile of rubble, doing a double-take. Looking at me looking at me. Nose to the grindstone. Nose grinding in the stone. I was so close to losing me.

I pulled my head up from the ground. Sloppy me. So easily succumbed to the lazy dumb. I rose my pose, straightened my back. Where I had slackened, all my credentials, all my principles, my earnest learnings, I gathered them up from the mud pile. Stretched them strikingly. Flipped them back and forth to see. Were they flexible, still stiff enough to stand with me, to go with me beyond?

I stood erect. Agile, I leapt forward, upwards. The biggest step outta there. That spring surpassing any dashes I'd ever made in the past.

I landed in the air. I'm still sailing. Somehow, I'd gotten clean in the process, the process of leaving the assembly line of manufactured chaos. I hit the end of that line.

In time, I remembered. Not at first, 'cause I was so glad to not recall it at all. But it briefly came back while I never looked, never even peeked in that direction, backwards. When you climb to the top of a mountain, and it is a hard climb, arduous, you don't look down. You look at the adjoining peaks that meet your view. The ones you couldn't have seen without this new perspective. You look at the sky, 'cause you're closer. And wonder how you can get even higher.

The Silent Partner

Ticket Master

Ticket Master. Dishing them out, doling them. One ticket for every ride into the illusion. You can stay as long as you like. It's a never-ending game. The one you lose yourself in.

You're lost. You're a loser. Till you figure your way out. The goal of the game is to find your way to the exit, to reside alongside the Ticket Master again. To thank him for the ride. The ride of your life.

One blink in his moment is an endless array of play in yours. Your playground, where you get to be in the circus with others, so many of them. However many the Ticket Master lets on the ride. Billions.

You're surrounded by others. Others like you, all wanting to play the game. Play the game their own way. They look at you. Some say friend, some say competition. If you unite together, all of you, you could greet the Ticket Master, stop the ride, all get off and know you've won together. But you think that would be impossible to achieve, getting all these people to agree, and it would end the fun of it. Wouldn't it?

The Silent Partner

He gave you some tips, some hints, some understanding. The rules that would help you out, help you explore with ease, help you build comrades, help you enjoy with peace this wondrous experience. He gave you some warning so you won't get lost in the maze. Dazed. Bewildered. Enemied. Wanting to leave.

You choose some of the tips and some of the cautions. Then, quite forgotten, you engage. Play. Someone says this; another shows that. You're led astray. You think it's more fun that way.

You slide into first base, second, third. You're on your way home. So many versions of home, you forget the only one is where you started from. The one where the Ticket Master is standing outside the ride, watching it, observing it. He doesn't alter the game, only plays out the rules. The consequences of your actions that led you to this or that, for or against the nature of things.

Some are walking around in a circle, a large one. They feel the commotion beneath their feet. The chiming of a rhythm they think they remember from somewhere deep. Perhaps it's the way out of here. When they start to want to leave, it becomes a longing to be freed. They take a few steps forward, then back. They haven't played out the results of their game yet. They've taken moves that have yet to move them into another place, to meet a new face, to race a fine car, to be a mother, to build a house, to rebuild after a storm, to survive a hurricane of rain, to kiss a girl, to feel heartache's pain, an uproarious laugh, a baby's pat-a-cake clap, an unexpected slap that's too hard hits home, but not the home where the Ticket Master stands. No. The one that makes them have to stay for a while, or longer. To see where that slap came from, to see who is behind it, to make it right and wrong again and again into the day and night.

You want to take flight, but what's the rush? There's all this fuss that you can fix. Harmonise under these blue skies – that fade to grey. The churning events of rock and roll that keep you hanging on – ignoring your soul.

Those who want to leave find a way; they end the charade. It's a battle of being neutral while playing the game, interacting while remaining still, coming back to zero. While the heavy sums of digits and gadgets clink and clack in your face, enticing you to bite. Hooked. You'd be caught again, only to want to be free of this beautiful ride, eventually. To master it, to stay clear not out of fear, but out of "done that, been there".

It becomes an obsession, both staying and leaving, when the need for leaving comes. The ignoring of the festivities while being anything but ignorant in attempting to leave. You start to see the Ticket Master in your dreams. You see him surreally mixed in with everything. He is the clown at the show, the rider on the horse, the tortoise who crosses the road, the scream in your wife's voice, the silence in the dark night, the red on the head of your freckled son. You see him as the key. The key to be free.

You don't want to implore anyone anymore, to get this or that. You don't want to run about. You want to find your way out. You're coasting, passing your pawn from one game square to another, taking in cash, tokens for later use. You take them as an excuse, just in case you need them for a while. You learn to smile. You see others. You think they're not like you, but yet you remember them waiting in line before this ride began. Déjà vu.

There are secret places in the scene. They lead you to the secret beyond secrets. They lead you to the door, and then the door, and another door till you open the exit. You follow them, the secret places and synchronicities that give you the key. At the same time, you mind your mind. It must keep time with the circus here and its entire spree, and yet hold the silence, concentrate to see what is behind this glee – this glee turned misery.

A glimpse of the Ticket Master comes every now and then. Sometimes you hear him speaking to you. He's helping you, while knowing you'll be fine when he sees you again anyways. It's the nature of the ride you take inside while thinking you are outside of it all.

Free fall…

The tunnel leads to your place of yearning. After you stop the needing and the jaunt of haunting woes that go along with happy days that stay for as long as a dream. It's the nature of the rules. The rules of nature. The cycle of the circle. The merry-go-round of town. Someone's pushing

The Silent Partner

the wheel in the opposite direction. It's me. Someone's moving too fast. Eccentric. Eclectic. Illusion of electric light. It's me. Spinning out of control, controllably. I stop this clock. This watchtower of power whose hands tick and tock, which seems so slow or much too fast for one's liking. The motion of each minute accelerated into a spin that threads the performance of us, the life we choose. We lose. We lose the game while we're in it. We lose it all, all our winnings. The only thing we take with us, to leave at the door – the final exit – is our ticket.

It's crumpled and worn, possibly torn. Or well-preserved, with only a few bruises, folded slightly to make it appear as good as new.

The Ticket Master doesn't take your ticket. He lets you keep it. He extends his hand to help you off the ride. You shake your head, maybe holding back tears, maybe full of bliss at being able to come back home. It's like you never left.

The Twilight Hour

In the twilight hour, things happen. That no one sees or thinks about except ones who want to. Notice. Nodding things. Things that don't speak, but say with gesture. Subdued communication that rings through the twilight hour.

I want to catch its spell. To devour it, albeit lovingly, into my soulful yearning. To see it from the inside out. To separate it from itself in dissection, to understand it in its entirety.

I hear the birds whisper it by name. Or maybe they said its name. I couldn't hear; it was such a quiet whisper that was not meant for me.

I tiptoe to the scene of the place where I think it may start. When the dusk rolls in and the stillness begins and the things that most don't think happen come alive. I wait for its energy to electrify me. It doesn't take long. It's me who's coming into its frequency. It is always there in the twilight hour.

There's a maze of haunting that spooks me easily. A chill of shiver that I know isn't coming from me. I want it to leave so I

The Silent Partner

can return to my comfort zone, but I can't bring myself to do so. It's me who needs to go. That which is here is always here in the twilight hour. I can't move myself out of this space. It raptures me. Subtly. I am tingling with its excitement. The warmth of its creeping embrace into every space. Within my bones, it seeps and rests, sits there. I hope to take it with me, to see it there inside of me. To know it's deeply buried there.

I hope it steals its way up to my heart. I hope it steals its way into my heart. I hope I see it going there and feel it press its entry and sink gently into opening, to let it in. I hope it never leaves. I hope it fills me with its shivering, its sleeping wakefulness that comes into me. How does something so invisible make one so invincible?

I hope it fills my eyes and moves to the sky of me, into my head, and clears out all the dread. I hope it fills me with its quiet, its dark that isn't dark, which seeps into me without breathing. Breathlessly it steals its way into me. That thing, that beautiful song that belongs in the twilight hour.

Merci

"Could I entice you to come this way, *s'il vous plaît*? To move to something rather untrendy? You'd stay with it so long that you would come to know it well. Relatively. Well, enough for you to see its value. With leaving selfishness behind.

"It is a tad difficult to leave the selfishness behind, because it becomes so appealing when you see what I will show you that you want the obvious benefits it brings. But the truth is, the benefits end when the selfishness takes hold.

"I want to show you how to make the world a better place. Not for me, but for you. I want you to see this so you will be gifted with its glory. It is my greatest glory, for you to be filled with glory.

"When you see the good that fills your basket to overflowing, there's no falling through the cracks anymore. It's all filled up. Every crack no longer that. Just ballooned into gentle folds that stop the escape of people falling through the blue halo into the darkness. Instead, they are caught in the stork's blanket, carrying them to a higher place where they become the great gifts to the world.

The Silent Partner

"I wonder if you will be open to see the beauty I could show you? The way to return the smile to the downtrodden man's face. The way to mend the cripple's back so he may stand tall and be the man he is on the inside, the man who wants so much to carry the burdens of his earth family on his firm spine.

"Can I take a few minutes, days, months, centuries of your time to use it preciously? I have some sights I think you might like to see, after you've gotten away from your current playbook. Here's a story, if you will. I hope it gives you a thrill.

"There once was a man who made his mother delight and his father proud. He raised fine children by being a gentleman to his kind wife. He took moments to focus on ways of well-being. He shared his labour with others and did so with love.

"His example became one of which others spoke fondly. He shook hands with his neighbour and strangers, and he smiled sincerely with each greeting. He never dismissed a chance to assist his fellow man, a lady in distress, or to wipe the runny noses of little ones who had gotten themselves into messes, tears running down cheeks and tears in their little pant knees. He lifted the babies who joined his society, and he treated them all as his own. He respected each one's way. He was learning, seeking wisdom without borders. He planted love where he went. He sowed it by setting it free, to make a better world. He carried life's burdens on his back and let them go with ease, as they pleased. Selfless, he was.

The Silent Partner

"I would like you to meet him. Would you take a moment now?

"Perhaps it doesn't matter right now. But if I could convince you, you'd thank me, I'm sure. But there'd be no need. I have no need for your gratitude. I only do this for you. I'd like to extend this gift unselfishly. I'd like you to meet this man. You might see him differently, then. You might recognise him in your eyes.

"You see, I saw him in you, when I saw you here. He is a version of you. I asked if he'd wait just around the corner, so I could bring him to you, if you so choose. He quickly complied because of the love in his eyes and his willingness to do a kind deed. Please come this way, if you do agree. I'll introduce you to the man of your dreams.

"He is a bit older now, though the youth in him has never left. He's excited to meet you, though he says he's sure he's known you before. He said you were the exploring type who left to claim your place in the world when you were very young. He wished you well, and if you care to take a minute now, he'd love to see you again.

"He gave me this token to pass on to you, his golden chain to link back to you. He's worn it since you left, though he said you were never too far from your home.

"Do you remember him now? Come. Here he is."

"*Bonjour, mon fils.*"

"Father. *Je t'aime.*"

"*Je t'aime.*"

"*Merci.*"

Pensive

The wall. Stood in my way. There was no way around it that I could see. Short of crawling to the top like Spider-Man. It is just like me to get a wall like this right in front of me. Immovable. Ridiculous. Obvious. Argh. Ugh.

It was white, blank. Stark. Staring back at me. Me staring at it. Head-on. Head-on collision. I'd like to bust through. But that was so like me, wanting to bust through. And that's it. Stopping there at its base, staring me in the face.

I'd like to say it was ridiculing me. To give me a reason for this pent-up frustration. I'd like to say it caused me to implode. Like I found the joker who put it there, and I had it out with him, or we had a good laugh over the prank he played. But that's not so. The joke's on me instead. I'm not big enough to push my weight around. To collide with this wall. To be the battering ram and punch it through, laughing triumphantly, shouting, "The joke's on you! Muahaha!"

No, that's not me. I'm not that forceful. That pensive me is trying to figure out how to get around this wall.

The Silent Partner

Maybe I should lean against it for a while. Pretend I'm just passing time while really pushing with my lean. Trying to weaken it, find its weak spot. Like it found mine by standing its ground.

Walled in. Welled up. I'm the cup half empty now. I have no reasoning that can make me jump this hurdle. Superman, save me now. Batman, send out the bat signal. I'm sending out the signal to you. Save me. I'm stuck in Gotham City with the Joker. The joker who has played this trick on me. Poor me. Who is the villain? Who is the victim? Who is the saviour? Who is the wall?

I bang my head gently on the surface, the blank white surface. I leave it there, resting in frustration. I rub my head back and forth, making friends with my enemy, affectionately. My hair climbs its surface. Fine strands dance, going upwards and sideways, spreading out against the abrasion. The friction between us eliciting electricity. We are strangely joined. Me with my hair, the wall with my hair. Now I'm stuck with its friction. I smooth my hair and pull my head away, and my hair wraps itself close to my neck. Hanging on to me tight with its loose might, maybe happy to cling to me, or maybe trying to choke me with the energy of the wall.

I put my back to it, the wall. I stand erect. Then slide down as my knees bend, and I drop to sit on my feet. Leaning. Always leaning against something. Pushing a little. Asking, expecting my enemy to support me so I won't topple over while figuring out how to defeat it. Let me defeat you while you support me. I don't think. I don't think because I never think I'm asking for this obstacle, because I am too nonchalant in coming and going to think about what direction that is, where I'm coming or going to. I'm travelling with runaway horses on a stagecoach to nowhere. Wearing the straight coat, the straitjacket tied at my back so I can't reach anything that might hurt me. I can just walk into walls. White ones. Blank, staring white ones. Staring at me, staring at them.

Give me a nugget, some little gem to get me out of this jam. The one I've got myself into without doing anything. Yes, without doing anything.

If you stand still long enough, you deposit enough dust that the powder forms a pile so high it reaches the sky. If a passer-by adds water, you'd be stuck in the mud. Mud hardens when it's left to harden. It creates a wall of time, locked into place by the pensive state of inaction – the life you want to live now expressed in fractional dimensions, proportions of minuscule degrees, a tiny opening to places you can go, trapped within these walls of you.

A Fisherman's Tale

Placidly I pace the space that I occupy. I wonder. What to surmise? I don't feel the pain the way you do. I don't see the rain as long overdue.

I am caught in the moment. The time at hand is at hand. I spread myself thin; extend myself to the brick and mortar of life, to build the building blocks of something worthwhile.

I am the freelancer. The one who catches the rainbow in his pouch but doesn't tell anyone about it. I let it go instead and let them believe it couldn't be had. They simply point and idly walk by, while the glitter is real gold. And there's more where that came from. Catch and release.

I cast my line as the fisherman of life. I fill my net with forget-me-nots that I never forget. I just let them go. Sometimes I spin the tale, the greatest fish story. People laugh with amusement. So do I. But I know it is true. It really happened. The gold is for the taking. Catch and release.

I find a pebble in my basket. It is round and awkward. Greyish brown, as pebbles go. I massage it between my

The Silent Partner

fingers, and oil it from my skin. Its rugged edges soften in my pocket. The flannel in my jacket lining hugs it gently, tosses it often. My fingers find it there, frequently.

We become a duo, The Rock and I. I call it The Rock, no longer a pebble. It got an upgrade. So did I. I start to smile a bit with it in my pocket. Like a secret. Not a dirty one. Not a little one.

Sometimes I pop it in my mouth and roll it around. It feels sound in my teeth. Gently rolling. Held under my tongue so I won't choke on it when I talk – though it would never do that to me.

I start to bulge. To feel good when I go somewhere. I start to transfer it from pocket to pocket. Jacket to jean. I start to feel heavenly. Golden. I start to call it a nugget. A nugget in my pocket. My secret piece of harmony. My Gold.

I think about tossing it. Gently, of course. Tossing it gently into a sweet spot so it can be in its sweet spot. Catch and release appeals to me. It goes away, though, just as easily – the thought. I hold on to it while letting it be loose in my pocket. But its time will be here soon. A place it wants to land.

People will walk by that site. They won't see its shine, its golden hue. They won't know its power. They will think that power couldn't be captured. They're looking for manufactured niceties, something they can hold on to that births an attachment.

I keep my secret, the clean, big one. I don't tell them about the rock that makes them feel powerful, that turns them into the God inside of them. I just let it go. Catch and release.

Eventually

Eventually, I cried. But it wasn't worth it. Crying is for change, not for things that stay the same.

I got the notion that this explosion meant something. And it did. It meant we were on the ride of our lives, rumbling into oblivion. The dumb oblivion. Not the one of genius with eye-catching beauty, the never-ending one. This one was going to end eventually. But it just seemed like it would last forever.

I cast a rock into the mould of the days I was sculpting in my life. These days. Cast a rock so I would remember I'd been here before. The rock would remind me. It would be the hard confirmation. The real, in the dream of not remembering.

I wanted to know where I was going and where I had come from. I wanted to stop the repeat, the treat of thinking everything was new and different and then – wham! – same old jam I found myself in. I didn't have that naive rush like in the old days, when I didn't care to stare into space and wonder where was grace, to free me from this cycle of defeat. Beginning, middle, end. Repeat.

I saw the glass bottle tilting on the ledge of the windowsill. It looked like it might tip over and spill. What would be inside it?

It had been there so long, dusty, standing in the sun with some residue inside, that no one looked within to see.

We thought it was just some scum. Likely it was, just dust and oil and soot that turned to scum. We thought so, even though we never gave it any thought.

One day it would fall. It would stop tilting and fall into the sink, where it rested on the ledge above. Or bounce, and go the longer journey all the way to the floor. Would it break? Would the paste inside come spilling out? Or would it just greasily stick to its inside glass, no longer transparent?

It needn't be transparent any longer. If it breaks, we get to see what's really inside, with all its shudder.

I took the bottle down from the ledge and shook it. Nothing; hardly moved. I wiped the outside gently and then held it at bay, to see if it would glisten in the sun. It did, some. I filled the sink with soapy water and placed its bottom in, slowly letting its open top sink down, glubbing water into it in gulps. I shook it about, poured it out, and repeat. I did it again. Repeat. It was coming clean from all the washing. I scrubbed some. Took a chopstick and poked it, long inside, and scraped from side to side, around and up and down. Repeat. It was cleaner now. Back to the start. Glub, glub, glub. Scrub, scrub, scrub. Then I flushed it with hot water to its brim. Again and again.

I was happy when it came out clean. I dried it off. It even smelled good, if it could. Clean glass. I wiped the ledge off where it had been. Squeaky clean. Gleaming. I put the bottle back on its ledge. After so many tries, I didn't have to surmise what the gunk that stunk was. So sticky you couldn't see through. Now, I knew. I knew its insides, even though I didn't see its guts go down the soapy drain. It still remained. I knew it was that sickly stuff. It was gone. After all those tries, it was done.

The bottle shone a prism across the room as the sun blazed through it.

Just Paint

An illustration of sorts. A writing of words with pictures. Cutting the cord of breath and entering death that is no more. Dying death. Absurd. An abortion of truth. Making death die. Then what is left?

Life. Life lifts me.

I draw the pictures in my mind's eye on to the canvas of this lesser life. It illuminates it with colour that it did not have before. I become the illustrator, the drawer of dreams. Illuminated in lines in between the pages of words. How absurd.

It makes me laugh out loud. It makes me want to not take it seriously. This uncovering of the mystery. This discovery of rhapsody.

I bloom.

I want to. I draw illustrations of petals of light and romance so bright it tickles my fancy. It tickles me. I am free. I want to be.

The Silent Partner

There is a painter that I know so very well, though her greatest secrets are kept incredibly within her shell. As they should be. She is she, not me. Except the many of me, the "me"s that make the One.

She is like the sun. She shines so secretly for all to see. She paints a disguise of eyes that see the portrait of the world we create, through masquerading days and parades of gaiety. Frivolity. I want it to be.

Painted, beautifully. Sacredly. Specially, with brushstrokes that only she can impose upon the roses. Because she knows. She wants to. She wants to know and understand and be sacred.

I rip the sheet on which I am writing and blow it in the wind. Like a paper airplane, it goes. I watch it flow. It lands here and there, whishing in the air.

A little boy runs to catch it. He uses his toe to hold it, stretching from his knee so gleefully. He looks at the funny writing. *Chicken scratch*, he thinks. But he sees the drawings. They illustrate the meaning that touches his heart. He thinks it is special. He wants it to be.

He picks it up, folds it gently and puts it into his little pants pocket. Here, he holds it for safe keeping, sometimes to take with him, so it's with him, and sometimes to put up on his wall in his bedroom so he can have a room with a view. Sometimes he holds it at arm's length as he lays on his bed, and then he turns it sideways and thataway, so that it can dance and make his heart beat, further into the deep. He wants it to. To feel the deep seep.

He likes the special day this picture of words came to him. It made him want to rub the world the right way. To make the genie come out of its lamp and grant him the three wishes that he saw in his heart. The three blessings that he could see in his mind's eye. The ones that he could paint precisely and brightly on to his canvas, of light.

Rose

I didn't want to leave you there, staring at the wall. The wall of life. But it was time. You were overdue, the coming out of you.

You expected it to be so. That it would come to this. I kissed you gently on your head as I rose to let you go.

It was me who was leaving. Leaving this paradise of roses filled with thorny branches that were too difficult to get around. It was me who was no longer grounded. Though I left you there staring. You were encapsulated with the sight before your eyes. It was like a piece of peace that never went away, though it dimmed when you distracted from it. You kept your gaze in this place. In that place of escape. Staringly.

Hauntingly, some would say. You looking straight that way. But what you saw was more than staring into space; space that they thought was filled with blank air.

I left you there because I knew you were in good company. You had figured it out, your way out. Out of the misery that was so prickly. You could smell the rose, and it led you to another and another.

The Silent Partner

There were no blunders in your epiphany. You were not caught in a trance that held you prisoner. The sights you saw were beyond constraints. They caught your gaze because they were so enticing, so enlivening, that the other side of what you were was less appealing now. Like deflated balloons from a party you missed but everyone still talked about.

You saw the way things are.

The staring stopped. I smiled back at you when you smiled at me. I didn't wonder why or what you saw, as the smile came so easily, filled with the intrigue of you. You rose from the chair you sat at and came close to me. I could smell your breath. It danced like the roar of the wind and the tossed ocean waves. You were brave.

Delicately, I was taken by the ecstasy you saw in me. I touched your hand that led to your heart, and you were fragile. The grains of sand that brick and mortar are made of.

I was proud of you, not like a boasting, but a love of completeness.

I saw you staring as I rose above you, and you met me there in your chair, right on the ground.

The Silent Partner

The Carpenter's Son

Carpenter's hands are the likening of the wood he crafts. The master craftsman. I feel the slivers as he touches the knit on my sweater. It catches like the twinkle in his eye does to everyone he meets.

I think it a marvel, but wonder would he not be better fit to be the environmentalist? Why the carver of the dead, that which was destroyed? From the hands of greed that feared too much to build houses in the trees and so slew the forest instead, to stand higher above it. Like the conqueror who crushes the peasant. This workingman conquers, with his hands, that which came from the land. The carpenter. He is one of those, I suppose. Yet he is the ancestor of Jesus, following in his footsteps, the carpenter's son, the son of the carpenter.

I wish for greater things, and yet they are all here. Laden in the dirt and the earth. The man who loves his son is the same as the original one. The man who loses his heart makes another feel when he sees him fall apart.

I am the storyteller of these things. I can take a piece, a small part, and make its case, but I cannot forsake its other perspective. The bad that comes out of the good. The good that comes out of the bad days we've all had. The way we choose. To stand, to talk, to smile, to weep.

I search for the dime in my pocket and think about ten times. The exponential times this dime will be tossed, dropped, picked up, thrown away or saved for another day at the bottom of some big purse. The shiny smile it will put on a young child's face when you tell him he can keep it, as what is lost by one is another's treasure.

I knit the unity between you and me with extending fingers that have no end. They keep sliding out of themselves with another ratchet, another hatchet, cutting them further from their origin. But it never fades away from where it started. Life's circle – a progression of concentric circles. A revolution of evolution, of each of us into all of us, into the One of *us*.

I love the woodsman now. He does his part to show us his example. We watch or participate with love or distaste. It doesn't matter which; it is our personal takeaway. We get to touch that piece of projection and put it in our pocket, to do with what we will.

Was I raised by a father of corporate greed? Chop down more trees, please. Was I a farmer's son? Till the earth until it's done. Sow more seeds, please. Was I a carpenter's son? Bring me more wood, please. What will I make with my wood today? Is it a cross to take Jesus away? Or will I carry it for my Father's Son? Whose son am I? Where is

the son I want as mine? What kind of woman have I been?
What man will I become?

The trees stand to show me their strength of stamina.
In unity, they forest themselves, roots entangled in the
ground across acres of land. I think I can end their time
with one small hatchet and many men, or few men and
powerful machines. They out-endure me. My greed, my
fear, my convictions, my offspring. They are okay to be
defeated by the mere force of me. They fall gracefully with
a force that shakes me to my core, so profoundly I have to
force myself to get used to the power they have over me.

I am meant to evolve. I am meant to understand. To grow
deep. To entangle into the many facets of me that make
this world a mystery. I must stand in the forest. I must be
the man I'm meant to be. I must become my Father's Son.

Trading Places

Say goodbye to the days gone by. The new way rises.

I am awed by the sight of you. From total darkness, you were covered, till into the new light you were rediscovered. The shining face of what you are.

I celebrated your coming-out party with a start, like the first beat after a heart attack. The thump that comes feels like thunder. The emphasis of a small common thing that is seen in a big light.

Gosh, what a sight to see. Victory.

You made it look easy. Just passing through, staying in the darkness with complete faith that this would come around. The sun would shine again, in you. You knew it would. You believed in nature. You knew it would do its job, and you'd come out from behind that black wall. You'd come out when it was time. Out from the dark that comes and hems in so tightly you'd think you were stitched to its witchery for dynasties.

You had faith. Not false believing, but knowing that grows from the course of nature. You kept keeping your

The Silent Partner

time, seeing the creeping darkness come. Patience. It kept coming. It consumed you. Covered you blind: 5%, 10%, 30%, 50%, 75%. You're all black now. Where has your lucky star hidden you? You can't find a clue to get your way out. Just hang on. The blackness lifts only after its worst. It's almost beautiful to be that subdued. In a vacuum of endless dark. Beautiful, like graveyards on scary nights, under a clouded skin when visibility is nil. Beautiful when you can endure it. The brilliance of holding on.

It started to pass. The good that came at 5% back was like that thump of heart after that heart attack.

The more it came, and the more you saw yourself again, was exponential in magnitude to how good you felt with this reprieve. You made it through the misery. The light of you peeping through was so bright we all wore our shades. You were vibrant.

I couldn't count the days that took you away. They were so dark we stopped counting. We thought it would seem worse, but it wasn't. It was just as long as the movement the other way. Our heads led us astray. Our nature. The nature of things has us beginning again and again, and our faith in the world lies only in how well we endure its cycles.

I saw you eclipse.

The Silent Partner

Living the Dream

He wasn't the type of person I would have chosen. He was too big, a bit too much, too large for me. But somehow it was a perfect fit.

I didn't dance much with him, not because of his size, but because that just ran out. We had our fill of the dancing from all the dancing we did when we were first together.

I tore into the pages of him like a well-worn story. One that most knew how it would turn out, predicting it all along, but leaving a twist of wit till the end, that they couldn't have, wouldn't have, and didn't guess – it ripped them open.

Time stood still while we changed. Days were like times and times again, and when we looked at pictures of ourselves we noticed the change. The face of someone we knew that was new. It was the old shots that didn't relate, the blank looks in our faces. We stopped taking poses for capturing moments on film and captured them on their own instead. Things got better that way. Like we were living the dream and choosing not the memory. That way we didn't have to remember, except when it struck us to do so.

The Silent Partner

I fondly did. I finally did. Tried to weave the shredded layers together without knowing where they started, and without the ending in sight. Some days it was worth scouting the memories out, some days it was nothing but doubt. Doubt that any of this followed a path of understanding where I might realise the bends that needed amends.

Time ran out. So I followed him to the grave without regret. He was grounded long before me, just like when we were living.

There was no screaming when it was all said and done. Nothing to scream about, and all was done. There was no screaming before it was said and done. What's the use of screaming? Just excuses for things gone wrong that you didn't do right. It's too late anyways. It's said and done anyhow.

I ploughed through the rest of my life without, when you were gone. It was like pushing dirt and dropping seeds that rarely sprouted. I did it anyways. I didn't know what would take or could take or did take, in any case, because I was too methodical to care. Not like sober disgust, just putting one step in front of the other so intently I didn't stop to see if anything was growing beneath my feet. I was uprooted; never planted my feet long enough to see where the road had brought me.

I don't know if I met you there. It seemed I was more airy still; you wouldn't have been surprised to find my head in the clouds anyhow. I was always there. My only stake was the hook I shot in the moon, trying to capture stardom on my way to heaven. Without bravado. Just footsteps plodding me along till my big show. My showstopper. The one where I landed in a place without gravity. The one where I followed you. After you left. After the years you were gone. The one I couldn't have, wouldn't have, didn't dream of when I was dreaming the end of this life.

I followed you home. Where are you, sweetheart?

Till death do us part.

Lila the Lily

Flowering petals caught in the beauty of God's creations. They unfold, each so slowly. Hours and days and weeks go by. Till they bloom. Like us, centuries later.

There is an eclipse that happens. Some say, "I started to wake up." Some say, "When I awoke." There is a turning over from night into day, in which nothing is as dark anymore. It is the unveiling of you, as you get closer to the light. The light is who you are.

Your soul sits quietly. Waiting. Watching. It's not the kind of waiting with wondering. Rather, it's the waiting with knowing. That what you are waiting for is going to arrive. To happen. To evolve. And then things will be more what they are. Easy.

I watch you bloom, though now you have not yet grown leaves, let alone blossomed. You are not yet rooted, even. Only dusty. Floating around without knowing that someday you will want to be planted.

To dig yourself into the earth, deep. To see what it feels like to begin to grow in your seeded seat. The dirt of the earth beneath your feet and the depth of your soul illuminating your way into the tillage, so fertile, you risk blooming early. But all in due time. All in dew time.

The revelations come one by one, like each new candle on your birthday cake. As you awake. The gifts you see, your new aspirations and inspirations, seem so unique. You wonder why, how, could you have been so trendy prior? So mired in following, without the unfolding of knowing that comes from your own insights?

Slowly you land into your own place. The bottom. Stability is your self. From here you grow downwards into roots, upwards into sky. The ascension seems slow. It is. In a matter of time.

Your perspective changes. Slowly. Shapely. Shifting you. It's a back-and-forth game requiring determination. Taking it. Persistence without resistance. Discernment. You must constantly choose to be the flower that you want to be.

The Silent Partner

Serenity

He rose again. To take a seat for evermore. I bowed to the strength I saw in his stature, even though it was hard for him to get up, to stand physically. He was so large just sitting there; he needn't have ever risen.

I was amazed and ashamed and perplexed, to have done the deed that got him up out of his chair. To move him so, to make him move. He rose and eyed me there, and took his direction towards me. All of it. His feet, his hands, his torso, but most of all his eyes, staring deeply into me, blue as can be. True-blue.

I waited till he reached me. Not to bow. I bowed as soon as he rose. Not cowardly or submissive, but purely out of respect. Out of pure respect. He didn't have to deserve it. It came with him; it *was* him. He owned it as he owned himself, and his stature told me so without a word spoken.

He directed his finger at me, his long fingers extending the endless extension of him. I froze in expectancy of something worth hearing, worth knowing. Life-changing phrases that would alter the stages of my existence and bore it into the depth of substantiality.

The Silent Partner

He didn't take his eyes off me. He didn't need to. There was nothing that mattered more than this moment, this altercation of substantiation.

"Up," he said.

I stood.

"Higher," he pronounced.

I bounced.

"Don't take life so tragically," he warned. "You are not cast for meagre ease. You are to hold the hand of the solidity that you cannot see. The mushroom that doesn't bloom is in the dark, where stark winds blow, and the soil holds tight with all its might to keep the things it needs deep down below.

"Stand," he said.

I lifted my head. To meet his eyes, and in them I saw myself aglow.

It was like the explosion of a thousand stars into one spark. Pure light. I was misconstrued into what I knew of me. I wasn't the shallow frame of mere existence. Rather, the butting force of a sharp edge so glistening I didn't recognise its cut, till I saw myself fall into pieces.

I was amazed, perplexed, transfixed. Changed.

How to rearrange myself with this new view. How to establish high ground in this time of change. How to be the wise one, like the One who stood before me.

I rose. I stood. I was the new him.

Eye

O Romeo, Romeo. O Love. Who are you? Friend or foe?

Bare your soul.

I saw through you. Your eyes are a different colour than mine, and now I know why. No two twos the same. Not set in a scene that everyone sees.

Your blues capture the world as an ocean. You see its motion, the smallest quiver in a blade of seagrass growing in the current. Everything is moving, or ready to, when you see calm seas. Your eyes are like nothing I've ever seen. It's been oh so long since I felt like I belong. I belong in you, with you. I belong, finally. I love your perspective on life, with this insight of you.

I tried the world on for size in your baby blues, and they fit like a worn pair of my best dancing shoes. I love you differently now. More like the soul you are, that is different from me, striking to see. Varied. Animated. Flowing. You make sense to me because of what I see that you see.

The Silent Partner

I see the world in browns, even upside down. It's earth that is worth its weight in sandstone. Stone on solid ground. I slip away, and you come to play inside my head for a while. You tell me you see the world like boulders through my eyes. Big stock of rock. Glistening grey that sparkles in the twilight. The sun is brighter, closer, bolder. Golden. In my brown eyes, you are as the mountain. Reaching up. Down. Suspended. Anchored.

Not like the casual anchoring of your boat that you float in your sea blue eyes, but anchored like iron and minerals and ore. Not like the oar you use to paddle your watercraft, but the heavy kind, the rugged bolt of metal.

You marvel at the sights you see in me. The sky is high but touchable, the mountains indestructible. Stamina. You lift the world; you are strong. You know why I belong. You feel like you belong when you see the world through my stare. You're loaded with care. You're grounded right here.

So who are you, my blue-eyed beau? You're not so different from the love I know. Your ocean oarweed tangles in my bare toes. You rock my boat when your honour glows. Into the world, you've brought the sun. Within all eyes, you're the Golden One.

We exchange glances between us. Our eyes meet. I know you. I love you. Seeing through to the inner eye of you, you are a mighty man to me. I am a wise woman, knowing you.

The Spirit in me bows to the Spirit in you.

The Silent Partner

An Offering
(Epilogue)

I walk to the ocean's edge because its lapping waves beg me closer. Its surging current washes me. I stand dry on the outside, but on the inside it fills me, cleansing both. I don't need any of the debris that it washes from me; even my most present thoughts stop and go somewhere, I don't care where.

It comes back to God. I do. The moment. The feeling. The cleanliness. The state of greatest escape. The lull in life, so still it is haunting, in the pleasantest ways of peace. I stop. And return.

This is yours, God. All of it. I have played the part of the story of stories that came through me, for you. I have chosen well and badly. I have seen the winds of change and thought that I could control them. Then came their rhyme and reason, the one beyond man's manic attachment. I see I am your instrument.

Then, I came to the water. Finally. And then it seemed like only a moment had passed since this lifetime began. And then only that same moment comprised of lifetimes and lifetimes since I was your spark. Your God spark. I realised. That is what is best said. I realised with my own eyes.

I give this all to you, to burn through me. This offering. All the woes and friends and foes and fleeting laughter and happily ever after. I sit and see inside and offer it all to you, back to you, for it is yours. Your play. Your stage. Your actors. Your world. A brilliant performance. I burn it back to you, in offering. Every experience, every feeling and every thought – back to you. I offer it all back to you, the full scene upon scene which I performed.

And then I bow. Not in arrogance or fulfilment, but in offering of myself. The last bow. I offer myself to you, the final cremation. I see the light of the fire. I return whence I came. The prodigal son. The story lent out to be played for a time, however long I took, however long or whatever way I chose to play it out, until it landed at your feet. You bore the idea. You put it into Mother's creating hands, and then out I came, the spark of soul to play, the son. And now I return it all. The play, the me, in offering, back into the light of Mother's shimmering hands, through the family circle, home to you. I am free.

Thank you.

The Author

Juliet Castle was born in a small prairie farming community. She began her life in grief at the age of one with the sudden death of her father. This led to a series of numerous death experiences, up close and personal, throughout her life. As an intuitive and highly introverted child, observing people, animals, and nature captivated Juliet. She grew insights into life's relationships, her inner being and the finer forces at work. Privately, she applied writing and poetry as an expressive outlet for communication to her self and to God.

The pinnacle of Juliet Castle's life purpose came forward with the accidental death of her teenage son. From here she delved, soulfully seeking, into her inner journey to find what truly lay behind life's veil, where she could find her son. In that holy place on that holy journey, what Juliet found was love. Juliet Castle resides on Vancouver Island, British Columbia, Canada, with her Romeo.

The Artist

Jaye Gray was born a yogi with a tiny crayon in her hand. Her first spoken words were, "I want to make a difference in the world." At eight months of age, when she could walk, she added a paintbrush to her crayon and set out to "make".

Today, Jaye creates soulful makings prolifically. Gray Jaye Studio is an outlet for all things playful, joyous and free – bold expressions in painting, collage, drawing, sculpture, illustration and unidentified makings are made with an open heart. Jaye Gray lives in Alberta, Canada, with her husband and two feline friends.

With Gratitude

I am deeply grateful to Jaye for her muse-like inspiration, keen eye, fine art talent, and unwavering encouragement, without which, this work could not have been enjoyably endured or completed.

My loving thanks to Peter Michael, my Rock, who unconditionally supported me, in all aspects of this writing, without understanding why or what I was doing, because I could answer neither.

My soulful gratitude to Jarvis. When you left us, my mind and heart were forever altered. In your youthful life and death I have learned from you what only a wise and ancient guru might have wanted to teach me. My gratitude for this gift is unsurpassed. My search for you has led to this writing. May it be humble, joyful, and life altering, by your example.

Juliet Castle

October 28, 2016